I. H. Anderson

Patriotism at Home

The young invincibles

I. H. Anderson

Patriotism at Home
The young invincibles

ISBN/EAN: 9783337303297

Printed in Europe, USA, Canada, Australia, Japan

Cover: Foto ©Andreas Hilbeck / pixelio.de

More available books at **www.hansebooks.com**

PATRIOTISM AT HOME;

OR,

THE YOUNG INVINCIBLES.

BY THE AUTHOR OF

"FRED FREELAND; OR, THE CHAIN OF CIRCUMSTANCES."

BOSTON:
WILLIAM V. SPENCER.
1866.

TO

ALL BOYS AND GIRLS WITH LOYAL HEARTS

This Little Volume

IS AFFECTIONATELY DEDICATED.

PREFACE.

THE leading title of this little volume was selected as the subject for a story at an early period of the late unhappy rebellion; but circumstances delayed the full accomplishment of the design until the present time. And while every loyal' heart wells up its overflowing thanksgiving to the Supreme Father of all for the blessed peace that now rests upon the land, still the writer believes there is to-day the same necessity for the exercise of an unfaltering *" Patriotism at Home "* as existed during the terrible clash of arms that shook the Union to its very foundation, and threatened destruction to our free and exemplary institutions.

Nor is it to the statesman, the jurist, the divine, the voter, alone, that this all-sustaining principle of a nation's existence is to be consigned, but every American Mother of the present day should instil into the mind of her child such a pure love of country as will prove a perpetual and invulnerable shield to the great heart of the nation in all time to come, for the destiny of this great republic may rest with the rising generation.

The characters who figure in the following pages are left in a measure free to perform their own parts, to fight their own battles; and if any one of them should be so fortunate as to "conquer a peace" with the indulgent reader, the result, it is to be hoped, may prove of mutual satisfaction and benefit. But if, in some instances, age seems to cast off the weight of years, and youth clothes itself temporarily in the mantle of maturity, the critic is simply reminded that when the battle-field claimed nearly all the able-bodied men of the land, the maintenance of patriotism at home, as a matter of necessity, devolved upon old men and young boys, loyal-hearted women and Union-loving girls.

Possessing certain knowledge that youthful "Patriotism at Home" was in nowise restricted to the "Young Invincibles" during the terrible struggle for our national existence, this little book is issued with a moderate hope that it may assist in perpetuating a pure love of country in the breasts of the young, while it shall prove not altogether devoid of interest to the general reader.

ROXBURY, September, 1866.

CONTENTS.

8   *CONTENTS.*

PATRIOTISM AT HOME;

OR,

THE YOUNG INVINCIBLES.

CHAPTER I.

YOUTHFUL PATRIOTS.

OM! Tom! have you heard the news?" cried a stout, firmly-built boy of fifteen to another lad of apparently the same age, as the two met near the entrance to a small white house on the main street of the village.

"News? No — what is it, George?" replied the stripling addressed, who stood in marked contrast to the other youth as regards bodily structure, for he was tall and extremely slender; but his flashing eye and quick movements indicated an activity that might in a great degree make amends for any deficiency in muscular strength.

"Why, Fort Sumter has been captured by the rebels, President Lincoln has called on the loyal states for volunteers, and the whole country is rushing to arms."

"Peppermint and shoestrings!" ejaculated Tom Sprightly, as he nearly brought George Herrick to the ground by the quick, nervous movement with which he seized him by the collar and turned his face to the west, as if to read the truth of the words he had just heard by the lingering twilight of the April day.

"Take care, Tom! Don't twitch a fellow down by any of your sleight-of-hand tricks. You know I'm clumsy, and can't always come upon my feet in falling, like you and a cat."

"It's lucky for you, my boy, that you put so many words between *Tom* and *cat*, or I should have taken offence at the comparison. But I ask pardon, George. I know better than to play any tricks on you. Now tell me, candidly — is this the truth about Sumter?"

"Yes, Tom, it is true; and the matter is too serious to jest about."

"So I think. But what are the particulars? How many were killed in the fight?"

"None killed on either side — so say the reports. Major Anderson and his handful of men fought bravely, and knocked Fort Moultrie all to pieces. But the barracks, at Sumter, were soon in flames, and it took most of the men to keep the fire away from the magazine. Finally, the commander decided to evacuate on the honorable terms offered."

"Peppermint and shoestrings!" again exclaimed Tom, impatiently. "Why didn't our government send Major Anderson more men in season? I don't see."

"It does seem strange that it was not done," replied the other; "but then I suppose the government knew best what to do."

"Well, this country is in for a big fight now, any way, George."

"I'm afraid so; but the South Carolinians commenced it themselves, and have aroused the whole North; so the *chivalry* must look out."

"If I were only sure these legs of mine would run the right way," said Tom, capering around his companion, "I'd stump you to enlist at once, George. They'll stand fire pretty well in the kitchen-corner, when aunt Huldah is frying doughnuts; but I don't know how they'd behave on the battle-field."

"Be quiet—will you, you jack-o'-lantern, and listen? Governor Andrew, of Massachusetts, has a regiment nearly ready to march, and he expects to have them in Washington in forty-eight hours. The other states

are hard at work, and ours won't be behindhand. As
for myself, Tom, I'm off in the first train Monday
morning for Boston, to enlist."

"Are you, though? But are you sure, George, that
Colonel White will give his consent? I don't see how
he is going to get along without you."

"Give his consent! Why, Tom, I should expect to
receive my walking papers at once, if I did not show
my readiness to enlist. I know, as well as you do,
that Colonel White has been in favor of doing everything that could be done with safety to prevent a war
with the South; but I know, too, now they have forced
it upon us, that he will consider it every one's duty,
who is able to carry a musket, to offer his services for
the defence of his country."

"How about your mother? Won't she have some
objection to make?"

"Not a word, if Colonel White favors the scheme."

"Well, is there not still a third person who may
want you to remain at home? Suppose Lucy White
should say, 'Don't go, George'—how then?"

"Come, come, Tom, none of that nonsense, if you
please," said George, somewhat sharply.   .

"O, I ask pardon," replied the other, a little mischievously. "But I'll tell you what, George, if that
nice little girl thought half as much of me as she does

of you, I should be the happiest 'Tom' in these *dis*-United States, and I would at once petition to have the other syllable hitched to my name, with an additional *s*."

" I see you are bound to have your joke, Tom, and there's not much use in talking to you; but you may as well understand now, that *I* consider myself— as I am— a mere boy, and have never had any serious thoughts about *any* girl."

" Fifteen years old, and never thought seriously about the girls! Why, I always took you to be a 'Young America;' but I shall be obliged to set you down as an 'Old Fogy.' Peppermint and shoestrings! I've been heels-overhead in love half a dozen times. And you'd better believe it's awful, I tell *you*."

" Stop your fooling, for once— will you, Tom? I have something more to say to you."

" Go on with your music— I'm all ears, as the donkey said to the organ-grinder."

" I was taken under Colonel White's protection about three years ago,— as you well know, Tom,— a poor, ignorant, good-for-nothing boy; and if I am any better now, it is owing to the kindness and generosity of those good people, one and all. I have been treated just as well as if I had been a member of the family, and have had all the advantages of a good

school, which I hope I have not wholly neglected.
Now, I think I can show my gratitude for all this in
no better way than by enlisting at once in my country's
service in this hour of danger, as I know Colonel White
himself would freely do if his old age did not make it
wholly out of the question.   You understand me, Tom.
So now for a talk with the colonel, and then an early
start Monday morning.   I am rather young, I suppose,
but am strong and tough, and my country calls me."

   " Then you are really in earnest about going, George !
Well, listen to *me*, now.   Just about a year ago you
saved my life, at the risk of your own, by rescuing me
from Squire Belmont's bull, whose fury I had aroused
by some of my foolish pranks.   I said to myself, at
that˜time, ' I'll stand by George Herrick as long as I
live' — and I mean to do it.   So, if you are going to
pitch into the rebels, I'm going too.   You can do the
fighting, and I'll do the running.   Peppermint and
shoestrings ! won't I show those rascally secessionists
my heels ? — after this sort ;"   and, throwing a forward
somerset, he brought his feet so near his companion's
head as to cause him to spring suddenly aside, with the
exclamation, —

   " Come, come, Tom ; none of your capers here, if
you please.   Just wait till you meet the rebels, and
give them a chance to shoot at you flying — for you

will never remain in one place long enough to be sighted."

" What are a fellow's legs given to him for, if they are not to be used? I should like to know," replied Tom, as he leaped over the fence beside the gate with the ease of a deer. " Come, now for a race from here to Colonel White's! I'll run round you ten times, throw six somersets, stand three times on my head, dance a hornpipe, chat with every girl I meet on the street, and report the news — of the war, not of the girls — to the colonel before you get in sight of the house. Come on, my boy!" and away the rattling fellow sped up the street, like a race-horse, in the direction of Colonel White's. But noticing that his companion continued at his usual gait, he soon came bounding back to his side again, exclaiming, —

" What a regular ' slow coach ' you are, George Herrick! Perhaps you don't like the odds I offered you for a race? Well, then, I'll throw in half a 'ozen more somersets ; " and over he whirled, like an experienced circus performer.

" What a confounded dust you kick up, Tom ! Why don't you join some circus or menagerie ? "

" The fact is, George, I did offer my services to one chap that came along here with circus and menagerie together ; and he took me on trial for half an hour.

But the plaguy monkeys were so jealous of my performances, that the man was afraid I would make trouble in the family, by proving to be the smartest one in the lot. And so, you see, I didn't get an engagement. I felt so bad about it that I turned somersets all one afternoon;" and over he whirled again.

"Well, you needn't turn any more here," said George; and he attempted to place his hand on the shoulder of his erratic companion.

"Guess not! You won't get that lion's paw on me in a hurry;" and the nimble youth was many feet distant in a moment.

"Upon my word, Tom, you are too bad. I really believe you would be full of your nonsense if you were going to a funeral."

"O, no; not quite so bad as *that*. You saw me at a funeral once, George, and I'm sure I wasn't full of nonsense then."

The tone and manner of the frolicsome lad were now wholly changed.

"Forgive me, Tom. I didn't mean to hurt your feelings. Don't believe me so cruel."

"Never mind, George. I know you didn't think of *that* funeral when you spoke. There's no harm done, however. I need a word once in a while to sober me down. But let me tell you, George, I do have some sober moments as well as other folks, and if I should give way to my feelings, I should be awful *blue* at times. I have no nearer relative than my aunt. I often think of the day when I followed my dear mother to her grave. I shall never forget it. I lost my best friend when my mother died. True, I have a good home at my aunt's; but no one can fill the place of that mother. George, I am sober for the present."

The two boys now proceeded up'the street, arm in arm, to communicate the war news to Colonel White, and to lay before him their plans for joining the volunteers.

The foregoing scene occurred in the old village of Harryseekit, a seaport town in one of the New England States, on a memorable evening plainly indicated by some portions of the preceding conversation.

2

CHAPTER II.

A SLIGHT DASH OF COLD WATER.

"WELL, George, what's the news this evening?" inquired Colonel White, as our two young patriots entered that gentleman's house, a few minutes after the family had risen from the tea-table. "I was just thinking that something of importance must have transpired, as you did not return from the Corner with your usual promptness.—Tom, take a chair."

"You thought right, sir," replied George Herrick. "The news is of the most exciting character; but I hardly know whether it should be considered good or bad."

"Indeed! What may it be?" questioned the colonel, in a most anxious manner. "I need not ask, however, for I have felt all along that Fort Sumter must fall. Is it so?"

"It is true."

"Any particulars?"

" Mr. Bayley has received three despatches from a friend in Boston, during the afternoon, giving a brief description of the fight, and finally of the surrender of Sumter ; " and George repeated the facts as already related by him to Tom Sprightly in the preceding chapter, with the additional rumor that the rebels were about to march on Washington.

" It is hard to feel reconciled to this," said the old gentleman, springing energetically to his feet, and walking rapidly up and down the room a number of times after the youth had finished his brief statement of the affair. " It is hard to feel reconciled to this," he repeated ; " hard indeed. — But what am I saying? It is all right — all for the best. Why should I doubt at this late day of my life? What do we short-sighted mortals know about it? Our heavenly Father ruleth all things for the best. We must wait patiently — and trust."

" It seems a terrible thing for men to fire on their own flag," remarked George.

" The strength of all governments must be tested sooner or later," replied the colonel, " and our fiery ordeal has come. Fort Sumter in the hands of the rebels, and the madcaps threatening to march on Washington ! Foolish, mistaken South ! Little do they dream of the vast military power that lies dor-

mant in the North and West, which this treasonable
course will immediately awaken. It matters not in
what light the leaders in the South endeavor to present the facts, — the position is a treasonable one, and
the whole world, ay, Heaven itself, will pronounce
their doom."

"The doom of all traitors, I hope," responded
George Herrick, with emphasis.

"Yes," continued the old gentleman; "it can be
nothing less. A president of these United States was
lawfully elected last November, in precisely the same
manner that all previous presidents have been
chosen, — by a perfectly free expression of the will
of the people through the ballot-box, as provided by
the constitution, — and they, a minority, at once set
themselves to work to disrupt and destroy the best government on earth, instead of acquiescing peacefully
in their defeat, and manfully preparing themselves
to try to bring about a change in the administration
four years hence! A scheme so utterly senseless,
high-handed, and base, was never before concocted by
short-sighted, impious man. Heaven grant that they
may yet come to their senses ere it be too late! And
this is the chivalric South! No; I will not believe it.
It is the work of a few discontented, aspiring dema-
gogues. The idea that the majority of the southern

people would, of their own free will, desert the constitution and the old flag, I cannot believe."

" Do you think, sir, there is any course left for our government now except to call for a sufficient military force to put down this rebellion?" inquired George.

"No, no; it is the only thing to be done now. Nothing else can save our republic. The rebels have invited the arbitration of the sword, and by it they must stand or fall. And there can be no child's play about it, either. The war must be prosecuted with the utmost vigor until every rebel lays down his arms and returns peaceably to his home. Then our government may *talk* to them — not before."

" Yes, sir; I think that is the way all loyal people will look at this matter," rejoined the lad.

" You are right, George. And they must not only look, but *act*. Let me see — I shall be seventy-eight in about ten days. Too old, too old, I fear, for any active service — am I not, dear?" said the venerable soldier, as he turned to his wife, a few years his junior, who had been a silent listener thus far.

"Yes, yes, my husband, I think you *are* a little too old to enlist. I hardly believe you would pass muster, even were you to dye these tell-tale locks," replied his amiable old companion, gently smoothing her husband's "silvered hairs."

" Yes, Colonel White, though you're very smart for your years, yet it would never do for you to join the army ; so George and I have made up our minds to go in your stead. 'Old men for counsel, young men for war,'" said Tom Sprightly, as he jumped up and marched across the room, with a ludicrous attempt at a military air. Halting before Lucy White, who was seated near her grandmother, he continued, " Don't you think, Miss Lucy, that George and I together would make a very good substitute for your grandfather?"

" Why, Tom," replied Lucy, mischievously, " if there is any running to be done, somersets to be turned, or 'peppermint and shoestrings' to be looked after, in the army, I think *you* would be worth a dozen grandfathers."

" And if there are any heads to be turned, or heartstrings to be broken," retorted Tom, in a mock indignant tone, "*you*, Miss Lucy, would make a right smart 'daughter of the regiment.' "

"Come, come," said the colonel, laughing, in spite of himself, " you two young rattleheads make sport out of everything. Tom, you young villain, come here, and stop your training."

" Stop my training, Colonel White !" exclaimed Tom, with feigned surprise, walking back to his seat; "why, I thought 'training' was the very thing that made good soldiers."

"The *first* thing a good soldier learns, Tom, is strict obedience to orders," rejoined the old gentleman, smiling; "and I command you to remain perfectly quiet for the next ten minutes — if it's a possible thing."

"O, that's easy enough; I kept still ten minutes and a half the other evening, when aunt Huldah set me to picking over the raisins for a plum-pudding," replied Tom, at once assuming a very serious expression of countenance.

"Now, George," said Colonel White, "I want you to tell me if there's anything in what Tom has just said about your idea of enlisting? Have you talked the matter over seriously, or is it only one of that madcap's jokes?"

"We have talked the matter over seriously, sir; and, as far as *I* am concerned, my mind is fully made up, and I want only your consent, to start for Boston Monday morning to join one of the regiments there, so as to be in Washington at the earliest moment. I have been thinking of this all the time this trouble has been brewing. I have no doubt that Tom is equally in earnest, though he always mixes up so much nonsense with everything, that one wants to know him as

well as I do to tell whether he means what he says or
not.   I think his heart is in the right place, but it is a
very crooked path that leads to it."

"If I wasn't under guard, George, I'd thank you
for that 'crooked' compliment; it's a good deal better
than none," said Tom, dryly.

"I give you your liberty now, Tom," said the
colonel; "only use it with discretion.   As George
and you seem to have acted together in this matter,
I shall talk to you both with regard to it.   But you,
Tom, will of course be at liberty to ask the advice of
those who have much more right than I to give you
counsel."

"I think more of your advice, Colonel White, than
of any other," said Tom, soberly.

"I admit, boys, that I am highly pleased with the
spirit and patriotism that have so manifestly prompted
you thus to step forward at the very earliest moment
to respond to your country's call.   I am gratified,
because it not only proves that *you* are made of the
right material, but it convinces me that where mere
boys show such spirit, there will be no lack of men to
stand by their country in her hour of peril.

"But, my young friends, notwithstanding I commend
this display of promptness on your part, still I must say,
decidedly, that I cannot give my consent to your enlist-

ing at this time. There are many objections to it, all growing out of this one — you are much too young. No one should enter the ranks under eighteen years of age. The bone and sinew have no power of endurance that can be depended upon at an earlier age. I had an opportunity to see the folly of having boys in the army during the war of 1812.

"Now, neither of you is much more than fifteen. It is not your duty to enlist; neither would it be for your country's good should you do so. But there are duties here at home that you can perform nearly as well as men, that will be of far more service to your country, probably, than anything you could do in the field; and these duties I shall be happy to explain to you at no distant day.

"And, boys, unless I'm greatly mistaken, this terrible war that is about to commence will last so long that there will be no objection, on account of your age, to your shouldering a musket. Then, you can do your country good service in the army; whereas, if you should enlist now, a few weeks' or months' service would completely break you down — thus depriving the country of your assistance ever after."

Both boys remained silent for some moments after the colonel ceased speaking. Evidently they had not been prepared for the opinion just expressed. They looked at each other a little uneasily. George was the first to speak.

"Colonel White," said he, "I am greatly disappointed. My heart was set upon this thing. I could not have given it up by the advice of any man but you. I have always found that you knew what was for the best; and I shall follow your advice in this case. But let me do all I can here at home for the benefit of those who *do* enlist, and to help the good cause."

"I am very sorry that you are so much disappointed, George," replied the old gentleman, in a sympathetic manner; "but I know you will, as usual, take a sensible view of the matter."

"And I, too, am much disappointed," said Tom. "I believe I was never so much in earnest about anything in my life; though George started the project, or I should not have thought of it, probably. But if he can stand the disappointment, I guess I can do the same. Somehow, I feel that I am pretty nearly right when I do as George does. I'm determined to do something, though, to tell against those rascally rebels. Peppermint and shoestrings! I won't give that up."

"There will be plenty to do here, and exciting work too," replied the colonel, "and I expect much from you two young patriots."

As the two boys were about to leave, Lucy White inquired, —

" How is your little cousin Mary, to-day, Tom?"

" O, she is nicely, now."

" I'm glad to hear it. .I think the croup is terrible."

" Yes, it is; and it runs in our family," rejoiced Tom, very soberly. " My great-grandmother died of it when she was about *two years old.*"

" O, you rattle-brain!" exclaimed the young girl. But Tom was off. " Do you know, grandmother," continued Lucy, turning to the old lady, "that Tom Sprightly is one of the kindest-hearted boys that ever lived, for all he is so wild? His aunt told me that he staid by her little sick girl's bedside one whole day and night, and waited on her as tenderly as she herself could have done."

" I know, darling, Mrs. French says he is always very kind; but he is forever playing off some of his pranks. He isn't much like George."

CHAPTER III.

AN OLD MAN WITH A YOUNG HEART.

OLONEL WHITE was fast approaching his
seventy-eighth year, and had been a resident
of Harryseekit for upwards of half a century.
He was an active, benevolent, straightforward man,
whose energy of character and unwavering integrity
had often placed him foremost in movements of public
interest. He had served his country with honor and
distinction in the war of 1812, when he entered the
army as a private, and won his colonel's commission
before the close of the second year of his service.
With a constitution naturally good, with habits of the
strictest temperance, united with a cheerful disposition
and a whole-souled benevolence, he was now, at this
advanced age, more active and enterprising than many
a much younger man. He was not wealthy, as this
word is generally defined; but there was a wealth of
contentment and benevolence in his truly Christian
breast, that shed little rays of peace and happiness

upon all with whom he came in contact in his every-day walks of life.

Colonel's White's residence was half a mile from the chief village of the town, known as the " Corner," on the county road. It was an old-fashioned one-story building, so spacious on the ground that his boys, years ago, whose sleeping apartments were in the northerly part of the house, always spoke of going up to " Burrville " — the next village — when intending to retire for the night. It was a substantial, convenient, and exceedingly comfortable dwelling. Everything was neat and orderly about the house and garden. The barn and other out-houses were noticeable for their studied good arrangements in every particular, which showed that their owner did nothing by the halves, and that the comfort of his domestic creatures was not lost sight of by him. His farm was small, in a high state of cultivation, and an appearance of thrift marked every part of it.

The house, standing upon land somewhat elevated, overlooked an extensive " Interval," a short distance to the east, through which glided two gentle streams of water, running parallel, and quite near each other; one having its origin in numerous springs, many miles away, while the source of the other was a large pond, situated in the upper part of the town. Both are insignificant streams, except in the spring of the year, when they sometimes overflow their banks, and become one sheet of water, extending over the entire length and breadth of the Interval, which abounds with stately elms.

The colonel owned a shipyard at a distant part of the town, and had a few thousand dollars invested in government stocks, so that he was in easy circumstances. His acts of benevolence, however, would have been creditable to a man of much greater means. No deserving person ever asked assistance of him in vain, nor was any really charitable object that came to his knowledge, however private, allowed to pass unheeded. He knew the secret of true happiness — *making others happy.* A simple rule, youthful reader, but it works out incalculable good.

Colonel White had raised a family of five sons, four of whom were still living, but all long since married, having families of their own, and residing at various distances from the old homestead, which was now occupied only by the colonel, his wife, and their granddaughter Lucy, a bright and cheerful little girl of twelve. But we will take the reader back something like three years, for the purpose of explaining the circumstances that induced Colonel White to become the patron of George Herrick.

At this time the old gentleman owned a young horse, a very fine animal, and generally well behaved, though, like most youngsters, he occasionally took a notion into his head to cut up some little caper, probably thinking it all harmless enough. However, no serious accident had ever occurred through any of his frolics ; and his master considered him perfectly reliable, although Mrs. White preferred the more sedate horse, "Old Noll." She said her bones were too old (she was five years younger than the colonel) to risk them by riding behind "Dancing Jim" — a name early applied to the colt by the old lady.

It was a pleasant afternoon in the spring of the year, and the colonel, having business down to the "Point," at the shipyard, harnessed up the colt, and invited his wife to take a seat with him in the chaise. The old lady, however, pleasantly declined the invitation, remarking that she would embrace some early opportunity to ride, when Old Noll was to be the motive power. So the invitation was transferred to Lucy, then about nine years old, who soon occupied the seat in the chaise beside her grandfather, having no fears concerning Dancing Jim, so long as she was to be partner in the dance. The old gentleman gave the word, and the colt was off in a moment. Mrs. White stood in the doorway a few minutes, looking after the

fast disappearing vehicle, and then, turning into the
house, said to herself, "I do wish my dear husband
would sell that young horse, for I never feel at ease
when he is driving him. He is a pretty creature, I
know, and everybody admires him; so I don't like to
urge the matter about selling him."

Dancing Jim behaved himself remarkably well over
the road to the Point — a distance of four miles —
showing no restlessness whatever, except when some
other horse attempted to pass him. This he would
never allow; and in this whim the colonel was very
willing to humor him.

Lucy enjoyed the ride very much; but then life was
all enjoyment to her. Why should it not be? Having
never heard aught but gentle and pleasant words between her grandfather and grandmother; having never
witnessed other than kind and generous acts between
themselves and towards their neighbors; and having
ever received from them the tenderest and most
thoughtful treatment, coupled with conscientious and
wise counsel, with regard both to her worldly and
spiritual welfare, — why *should* she have been other
than a pleasant and happy little girl, imparting pleasure and happiness to others? If her grandparents —
who certainly must be experiencing some of the in-
firmities of advanced age — could be almost uniformly

cheerful and pleasant, why should not she be happy, and thankful to her Maker, blessed as she was with youth and health, and surrounded and cared for by the kindest of friends?

Lucy was an orphan, it is true; bu̇ parents died when she was so young that she never̤alized her loss. She. was the only child of Colonel Wh youngest son, who died when Lucy was about two years old. In less than a year her mother, also, was buried; and the little orphan was thus early left in the charge of her grandparents. But Lucy was not spoiled by this disposal. Far from it. The truly good old couple fully realized the weight of their charge, and faithfully performed their duty, as parents and Christians, towards their little granddaughter.

But to return to the ride. A little over half an hour brought them to the shipyard; and, while Colonel White was attending to his business, Lucy interested herself in watching the ship carpenters, in their various labors upon the vessel on the stocks, in process of construction. She had visited the shipyard a number of times before; but she had never seen so large a vessel wholly out of the water, and was surprised at the massiveness of the structure. It was a ship of nearly a thousand tons. Whilst she stood wondering how the large timbers had ever been

3

put into their proper places in the ship's hull, a dozen
or more of the workmen came along near the spot
where she was standing, and, stooping, all together
took hold of a long and heavy piece of timber, that
lay upon ⬛ ground; when, at the word "now," they
lifted it with perfect ease, placed it upon their shoulders,
and marched off with it to another part of the yard.

At this moment Colonel White came up to Lucy,
in company with the master workman, having trans-
acted the business that brought him to the shipyard.
The little girl directed his attention to the men who
were walking off with the stick of timber, saying,—

"I've been wondering, grandfather, how they put
such great timbers as I see in that ship's frame into
their places; but it is all plain now."

"Yes," replied the old gentleman, "'in union there
is strength.' Now, those men, individually, could have
done nothing with that large timber; but all together
they can do with it as they please. So with this
blessed country of ours. The states, individually, are
weak and powerless; but united, they are a powerful
and prosperous nation."

"I think I see now, grandfather, better than I ever
did before, what you mean when you talk about the
'strength of the Union.' I guess it's when the people
of all the states keep together, and *lift* at the same

time, just as those carpenters lifted the piece of timber."

"That's it, exactly!" exclaimed the colonel, delightedly, who never let an opportunity pass unimproved of imparting to the young a love of coun⬛ "But I fear that at this very moment some men are so foolish, or wicked, as to advise the states to '*lift*' one by one; but should this unwise step ever be taken, some of the weaker ones will be sure to *break their own backs.*"

CHAPTER IV.

A YOUNG BOY WITH AN OLD HEAD.

COLONEL WHITE and Lucy were soon re-seated in the chaise, and Dancing Jim was making good time on his way home. They had proceeded less than half a mile, when, on approaching a frame building that had been recently erected, and on which three or four men were at work, he began to prick up his ears, and show his propensity for " dancing" — started, probably, by the glancing sunshine upon the newly-hewn timbers of the frame. The colonel spoke coaxingly and gently to him, and he seemed to be recovering from his fright; but when they were directly opposite the building, one of the men threw down a long, wide board upon a pile of the same material, making a loud, sharp report. This was too much for the nerves of Dancing Jim, and, seizing the bit firmly between his teeth, he was off in a moment, at the speed of a locomotive.

The old gentleman always kept his carriage and

harness in the very best order, and consequently he
felt safe in that respect, if he could keep clear of col-
lisions. He hoped to be able to retain sufficient control
over his horse to guide him in the road, if nothing
more, and braced himself for that purpose, cautioning
Lucy, at the same time, to remain quietly in her seat,
and to hold firmly by the strap at the side of the
chaise. By pulling suddenly and alternately on one
rein and the other, the colonel endeavored to wrench
the bit from the horse's teeth back into its proper
place. But the animal's jaws were set as firmly as a
vice, and he could not accomplish the object. Colonel
White glanced anxiously at Lucy; but the little girl
behaved remarkably well. She neither screamed nor
troubled her grandfather by catching hold of his arms.

The highway was smooth, broad, level, and, for
something more than a mile, nearly straight; but this
portion of the road they were passing over almost with
the swiftness of the wind. At the termination of the
distance named, the road turned suddenly to the right,
and a brook was crossed by a short wooden bridge.
As they neared this point, the colonel began to feel
uneasy, fearing that the horse might not make the
turn, or, if he did do so, the suddenness of it would
overturn the chaise. The people looked aghast from
the doors and windows of the occasional houses which

the horse dashed past; and the few pedestrians on the country road mostly sought safety by nearing the fence at one or the other side of the highway. One or two men, more daring than the rest, made slight attempts to stop the career of the horse; but they might as well have tried to check the rushing whirlwind.

On sped the excited animal; and now the turn of the road was nearly reached. But, at a short distance in advance, Colonel White and Lucy saw, at the same moment, a stout boy, apparently of about twelve years of age, with a fishing-rod in his hand, climbing nimbly over the fence at the side of the road nearest the brook. He sprang from the fence, ran swiftly across the road, threw down his fishing-rod, turned, and placed himself so as to be on the nigh side of the rapidly approaching animal. The colonel saw, at a glance, that the boy was determined to make the attempt to seize the horse's head, and barely had time to exclaim, "Heaven protect you, my noble boy!" when he felt, by the strain on the reins, that the animal's head had been drawn nearer the ground, and saw that the lad had both hands firmly hold of the bridle, near the bit.

The horse continued his mad career; but, after a few bounds, there was a perceptible diminution in his speed. The weight of the boy — for the headlong

DANCING JIM IN CHECK. — Page 38.

course of the horse took him completely off his feet — soon began to tell upon him. They were now at the bend in the road; but the old gentleman was satisfied that it would be extremely hazardous to make the short turn, even if he should succeed in guiding the animal in that direction, and he instantly decided to let him go straight ahead upon the side of the highway, as the gutter was not deep at this point; and he was confirmed in this decision as he heard the manly voice of the boy, " Slack the rein, and let him run straight for the fence ! "

The speed of the horse was so much slackened that the boy had recovered his feet, and had now, evidently, some control over the animal. One bound more, and Dancing Jim brought up against the little embankment near the fence, with his head between the two lower rails, and the ends of the chaise-shafts imbedded some inches in the loose earth.

Colonel White, who had his feet well braced against the front part of the chaise, remained in his seat; but Lucy, who, in the excitement of the moment, had quitted her hold of the strap, was thrown forward out of the chaise. The boy, however, it would seem, had anticipated something of the kind, for he turned in season to catch the little girl in his arms; and, although the great force with which she was precipitated upon him was sufficient to bear them both to the ground, still they received not the slightest injury.

The old gentleman instantly jumped from the carriage, and, having satisfied himself that none of the party were injured, grasped the boy cordially by the hand, and warmly thanked him, over and over again, for the good service he had rendered them.

They now turned their attention to the runaway. He had lain perfectly quiet from the moment his career was so suddenly cut short. He could not well be otherwise than quiet, as his neck was firmly fixed between the rails. With the assistance of the boy, who appeared extremely cool and self-possessed, the colonel loosened such portions of the harness as the case required, and ran the chaise back. Then, by standing upon the lower rail of the fence, he sprang it down sufficiently to enable Dancing Jim to withdraw his head with perfect ease.

The moment the horse's head was released, the lad seized the bridle, and gave an encouraging word, when the animal quickly sprang to his feet. He had received no injury, except a scratch on the side of his head, where it had scraped against the rail. He had evidently been greatly excited and alarmed, for every fibre in his body was quivering like a lump of jelly.

His master talked to him kindly, patted him, and gently rubbed him with his hand, which had the effect of soothing him greatly.

" Well, Lucy," said the old gentleman, after a few minutes thus passed, " shall we tackle up the colt again, and start once more for home? or what shall we do?"

" If you think it is safe, grandfather, I guess I won't be much afraid; but —" and she cast a furtive glance at the boy by her side, as if she thought that one so brave as he might have something to suggest to help them out of their difficulty.

" I've been trying, ever since the horse stopped," said the boy, without the least hesitation, "to think what's best to be done; and it seems to me, Colonel White, that it wouldn't be exactly safe for you to put that skittish colt into the chaise again; but you've got another horse at home, and if you'll trust me, I'll ride this young one up to your house, and bring the old horse back, and you can tackle him up, and get home before dark."

" Very good advice, my lad, and I thank you kindly for it," replied the colonel, with a smile; "and I will accept your offer upon two conditions: that you will allow me to pay you well for the trouble, and that you will now inform me to whom we are

indebted for our present safety. You know who I
am, I see."

"My name is George Herrick. My mother lives
right back here, in the last house you passed. You
may pay her what is right for my going after your
horse: she needs it. If you'll just take my fishing-
pole in your hand, and walk to the house with your
little girl, I'll soon be back with your other horse.
The chaise will be safe enough here at the side of
the road, I guess."

Colonel White removed the harness from the colt,
and put it into the chaise, and, taking a small blanket
from the box, he placed it upon the animal, instead
of a saddle; and George Herrick instantly mounted.
The colonel was pleased to see that the boy was a
good horseman. Tearing a blank leaf from a mem-
orandum book, the old gentleman simply wrote,
"Dear wife: Allow this boy to 'swap horses'—all
well;" and signed his name. George took the note,
and Dancing Jim was at once on his way homeward,
at a smart trot.

CHAPTER V.

THE COLONEL MAKES A PROPOSITION.

THE old gentleman and little girl soon reached Mrs. Herrick's. They stood in need of no introduction, for the colonel had passed to and from the shipyard so frequently during a period of years, that he was well known to all the residents of that part of the town; and Mrs. Herrick had recognized him and Lucy as they were whirled past the house a short time before by the runaway horse, and expected to hear of some accident happening to them. And now, as they approached the door, she met them, and anxiously inquired if they had received any injury.

" No, madam, we have not — thanks to your brave son, who risked his life in our behalf;" and the colonel related the circumstances as they are known to the reader.

Mrs. Herrick listened with much interest, and when Colonel White had concluded, she exclaimed, fervently, —

"Thank Heaven that none of you were hurt! I know George is somewhat daring; and I've often told him that if there's any danger near, he is sure to be in it. But I'm right glad if he has been of any assistance to you, Colonel White."

"Any assistance to me! why, he has probably saved some of these old bones of mine, and perhaps some of these young ones too," replied the old gentleman, as he affectionately placed his arm around his little granddaughter.

They had followed Mrs. Herrick into the house, and taken seats, to await the return of George. The room was small, and plainly furnished, but everything was neat and orderly, which showed that the occupant was a woman who could make scanty means go a good way towards keeping up a decent exterior appearance in household arrangements. Her own person and dress were equally unexceptionable.

Colonel White knew something of the history of the family. He knew that Captain Herrick had borne the reputation of being a spendthrift; that it was generally believed that he had squandered, in some way, a handsome little property which his wife inherited from her father, and then, when the gold excitement was at its height, suddenly departed for California with some of the early adventurers, and had never returned.

The colonel now felt such a lively interest in George, who had just rendered him so good a service, that he thought he might with propriety make some inquiries with regard to the circumstances of the family; which he proceeded to do.

Mrs. Herrick knew the character of her visitor well enough to feel satisfied that it was no idle curiosity that prompted the questions, and she candidly informed the old gentleman that Captain Herrick had done nothing towards the support of her and her boy (George was an only child) since he went to California, and that she had heard from him but once, and then by mere chance, as he had never written to her.

She continued to say that she had sometimes found it rather difficult to obtain the necessaries of life, but still had managed to get along, after a sort, without giving up her claim to the little house and acre or two of land where she lived. She seemed to lament, more than anything else, that her son was growing up without any permanent employment, and without education; for since he had been old enough to help her, she had been obliged to keep him from school so much of the time, that he had fallen far behindhand in his studies, and finally felt so much ashamed of his ignorance that he objected to go to school when he had the opportunity. She said George was high-spirited, reserved, and rather inclined to gloominess at times; that lately, although he was always kind and obedient to her, this unhappy state of mind seemed to be growing upon him; and although she felt quite anxious with regard to the matter, she could not divine the cause.

Colonel White had listened attentively to the foregoing statement, and immediately said, kindly, —

"Mrs. Herrick, I feel much interest in your son, and think I can assist him, and you, too, in a manner that neither of you will object to. I will make a proposition, and leave it for you and George to think over, and when you have come to a decision, you can let me hear from you. It is this: I own a small house, quite near the one I occupy, that is convenient for two small families. Uncle Bill Ballast and his wife are the only occupants of it at present, and a kinder old couple are not anywhere to be found. Now, the other part of the house, I think, will be just the thing for you and George. I propose that you remove there without delay, and let this little place, as you are too far from the village to obtain any remunerative employment.

"The advantages of such an arrangement, I think, you will at once see: you will be very near the village, and having the reputation of being a good seamstress, you can obtain all the needlework you wish. In fact,

my wife will want you to assist her quite often, for
although our own family is small, she is always making
up something for some of our grandchildren, or for
somebody's grandchildren. Then George will be in a
different school district, and will probably not have the
same objections to going to school that he has here. I
think I can make that matter right. And I agree to
find employment for him all the time he is out of
school, if he wishes to work, and will pay him well
for what he does. ' Uncle Bill' works for me the
most of the time, but I often need somebody else.
Now, madam, you can think this matter over, and
decide at your leisure."

" Colonel White, I cannot express to you my gratitude for the interest you take in the welfare of my
son," replied the lady, affected to tears, " and for the
generous proposition you have made both with regard
to him and myself. I shall talk to George on the
subject without delay, and think I might now safely
say that we will accept your kind offer. May Heaven
bless you for your goodness ! "

" Don't be hasty in making up your minds," rejoined the colonel ; " weigh the subject well, so there
may be no regrets afterwards. I hold myself ready on
any day to perform my part of the agreement."

" Are you certain, sir," asked Mrs. Herrick, with

some hesitation, "that Mrs. White will like such an arrangement as you propose?"

"Don't give yourself any trouble on that account," replied the old gentleman, with a smile. "Although wife and I have ever made it a rule to consult each other's wishes, even about what some might consider trifling matters, when it can be conveniently done, still we have as uniformly acted upon our own individual judgments and inclinations when circumstances rendered it necessary; and long experience has convinced us that we have pursued the proper course in this respect. Should we enter into this proposed arrangement, I think you will discover that Mrs. White will strive all the more to make everything pleasant, from the very fact of knowing that it is a favorite project of my own."

"Ah," exclaimed Mrs. Herrick, with a sigh, "I fear all husbands and wives do not understand the secret of domestic happiness so well as you and your kind wife do."

"Having had an experience of over fifty years," rejoined the colonel, "we certainly ought to be able to walk in the paths of peace and happiness together by this time."

"Here comes George with Old Noll tackled up all nicely in the chaise," exclaimed Lucy, who had been watching from the window for the last half hour. "What a smart boy he is, to stop and get the chaise as he came along, instead of riding home first on horseback! You didn't ask him to do so, grandfather."

"No, my dear, for I was well convinced that he would do so without," he replied. "He showed the coolness and thoughtfulness of a man in all he said and did; so I let him take his own course. And now, Mrs. Herrick," continued the old gentleman, as he turned towards her, "there is a little matter for me to arrange before I leave. I consented to let George go and exchange horses for me, on condition that I might be allowed to pay well for the favor, and he told me to pay you instead of him. Now, I am going to look at the whole matter in a business light. If he had not so bravely stopped my runaway colt, undoubtedly my chaise would have been broken, and the colt, perhaps, badly injured, which would have been no small loss to me — not to speak of the risk to Lucy and myself. I know by your son's manner that he would not accept pay for saving my limbs or life; but you can and must accept this on account of his saving my property;" and he placed a ten-dollar bill in the poor woman's hand.

"Thanks, thanks; I *will* take it, for I am in need—

4

and I know it is cheerfully given. May Heaven reward you as you deserve ! "

By this time George had driven up to the door, where he was met by his mother and her visitors.

" Well, my son, did you get the young horse home without any trouble?" asked Mrs. Herrick.

" Yes, mother, he was gentle as a lamb."

" Was Mrs. White alarmed when she saw you with the colt?" inquired the colonel.

" No, sir ; I thought she might be frightened if I rode right up to the house ; so I stopped a little short of it, hitched the horse, and then went and told her that you were safe, and gave her the note you wrote."

" You were very thoughtful in doing so," replied the old gentleman, more and more pleased with the intelligence of the boy; " I did not think to caution you about it before you started. But you did just right."

Colonel White and Lucy were soon seated in the chaise, and when ready to start, he said, —

" George, I shall consider myself under a lasting obligation to you for what you have done this day. Perhaps my old bones were of no great consequence, but my little girl here was in danger as well. I know she feels very thankful to you, although she has not said so. How is it, my darling?"

" Why, yes, grandfather, of course I thank him

very much ; for if you had been badly hurt, or killed, I should have cried myself to death. I do thank you, George Herrick," — and she looked him directly in the face, — " and I never shall forget that you quite likely saved my dear grandfather's life."

" I'm glad I happened to be there," replied the boy ; " but then anybody ought to try to stop a runaway horse."

" Well, George, I have been talking to your mother about making some sort of a bargain with you to work for me," said the colonel. " I hope you will make up your mind about it, and come and see me before many days. Till then, good by. Good by, Mrs. Herrick."

Old Noll now started off to fulfil the engagement that had been so recklessly broken by Dancing Jim — that of taking his master and little mistress home. This he did with safety in his own good time, and thus proved the truthfulness of the adage that " slow, but sure," is often the best policy.

CHAPTER VI.

THE COLONEL AND HIS WIFE.

A S Colonel White led Old Noll into the stable, that ancient piece of horse-flesh cast a reproachful glance towards Dancing Jim, snugly ensconced in his stall, as much as to say, " See what a journey you've made my old, rheumatic limbs perform by your youthful folly. When will you learn to exercise common horse-sense, and not be frightened at every little clatter that assails your ears?" But the young horse at the moment had his head buried up to the eyes in a heap of sweet clover that Uncle Bill had placed before him a short time before, and consequently took not the slightest notice of the suggestive look that his venerable companion had bestowed upon him. Had he been aware of the thought that his master was entertaining at the moment, perhaps he would have shown more concern for his reprehensible conduct that afternoon.

Lucy had explained to her grandmother, while her

grandfather was caring for Old Noll, all that George Herrick had omitted to do, so that when the old gentleman entered the house, no allusion was made to the ride; but a pleasant greeting of words, a cheerful smile, and a warm pressure of hands showed that the affectionate old couple were both happy and thankful that the affair had terminated without serious accident.

After tea the colonel said to his wife, somewhat abruptly, —

"My dear, I've made up my mind to dispose of that colt. He'll break somebody's neck yet."

"I've always considered him dangerous, you know," replied Mrs. White. "But what do you intend to do with him?"

"I scarcely know. If I offer him for sale, of course I shall have to say that I sell him because I consider him a dangerous animal, and that would be such a poor recommendation that he would not bring half his value; besides, it would not be *right* to sell to another a horse that I was afraid to drive myself."

"I see, my dear, that would not be up to *your* standard of just dealing. But is it not wholly on my account that you propose to dispose of him at all?"

and the old lady looked earnestly into the face of her husband.

"That is the main reason, I candidly admit," he replied. "As for myself, I should not be afraid to drive him again to-morrow; but I know you have always been somewhat uneasy about me when I am away with him, and you will be more so now than ever before. So I've made up my mind to dispose of him in some way."

"He is truly a handsome creature, and I dare say he will make an excellent horse," returned Mrs. White. "I know, further, that you think a great deal of him, and would like to keep him, if you could do so and feel that you were doing right. So don't think anything more about selling him at present, and perhaps he will become steadier of his own accord when he is a little older. Only promise me you will not drive him again till we all think it is safe for you to do so."

"I cheerfully promise that I won't drive him again till you, my dear, are perfectly willing to accompany me. In fact, I have been cruel to do so ever; but I thought you were a little too careful."

"*You* cruel!" responded his old companion, as she affectionately placed her hand upon his arm. "When you *are* cruel there will be no such thing as kindness this side of heaven."

" And the man that would, intentionally, be cruel to *you*, my dear wife, could not appreciate even the kindness of heaven."

" You wouldn't know how to *begin* to be cruel, my husband," said she ; " so don't name the word again, I entreat you."

" And what thinks our little Lucy about selling the colt?" asked Colonel White, addressing himself to the child, who was busily engaged with a book at the other side of the table.

" Sell the colt!" exclaimed Lucy, quickly looking up. " O, I don't want him sold; but I hope you won't drive him any more till he knows how to behave himself. He was very naughty this afternoon."

" Yes, he was indeed," replied her grandfather, "and I don't believe we can trust him again. I guess we shall have to sell him."

Lucy left her seat, and went round the table to her grandfather. Placing one arm about his neck, she smoothed back his long, white locks with the other hand, and imprinted a loving kiss upon his broad, white forehead, saying, —

" Please don't sell Dancing Jim!"

" Why not, darling? "

" O, I'm afraid if you sell him because he is naughty, that you will sell *me* some time ; " and she looked archly into her grandfather's face.

" Sell you? I don't believe we could find anybody that would buy you ; " but the manner in which she was pressed to the old gentleman's bosom plainly told the little girl that there was no danger of her changing hands at present.

" I don't suppose any one would want to buy me, grandfather ; but then *I* never ran away with anybody, and almost broke their necks, as the *colt* did."

" No, you never did, deary ; but then I suppose you will be likely to break somebody's *heart* one of these days." The old gentleman exchanged smiles with his wife.

" O, I'll never break *anybody's* heart," said the child, understanding the observation literally, " for that would be just as bad as to break a neck."

" Well, dearest one, I guess we shall not sell either you or the colt at present ; so you need not be troubled about the matter." Her grandfather tenderly kissed her, and she went back to her book.

" What did you think of the lad who rode the colt home and took the old horse away this afternoon? " asked the colonel of his wife.

"I thought he appeared like a smart boy," she replied; "but he did not tell me that *he* stopped Dancing Jim — that I learned from Lucy before you came in. So the boy is modest as well as brave."

"I think he possesses many good qualities, and that he only needs proper training and education to make him, when he arrives at manhood, respected and honored."

"And what do you propose to do for him?" inquired Mrs. White, as if it was a matter of course that *something* was to be done.

"How do you know I purpose to do anything?" returned her husband, with a smile; "has Lucy said that I do?"

"No; she merely said that you had a long talk with the boy's mother while you were waiting for the horse, but she did not know what it was about. *I* know, however, that a person who does Oliver White a favor never goes unrequited — especially if that person be a boy who risks his life in performing such a service."

"And what would my wife say if I should tell her that I had already made such arrangements with regard to the future of that boy as would involve her coöperation in a guardianship over him until such time as he should arrive at years of discretion?"

"I would say I was certain that my husband could never make any arrangement, especially in a matter of this kind, in which I would not only cheerfully acquiesce, but earnestly assist in doing all that I could for the gratification of the one and the welfare of the other."

"Spoken like my own dear wife, as you are," said the old gentleman, affectionately.

The colonel now proceeded to inform his wife as to the exact proposition which he had made to Mrs. Herrick, with regard both to her and her son — all of which arrangements Mrs. White cheerfully assented to. She was very much pleased with the idea of having Mrs. Herrick for a next-door neighbor, with the privilege of calling upon her for assistance as often as needful. Although not very well acquainted with her, yet she had always heard her well spoken of by those who knew her best. Her reputation was that of a smart woman, who could turn her hand to almost anything in the way of household matters, and one who possessed good sense enough not to pry into other people's affairs; and Mrs. White said to herself, "How nice it will be to have her so near!"

When Colonel White and his good lady retired that night, having completed their little plan for the assistance of the poor woman and the welfare of her boy, it was with far deeper satisfaction, and happiness, we venture to say, than many a man experiences who has made his thousands in a single day by speculating in " petroleum," or by clothing our noble soldiers in miserable " shoddy."

CHAPTER VII.

MOTHER AND SON.

AT the same time that the discussion related in the preceding chapter was going on at Colonel White's, Mrs. Herrick and George were earnestly engaged in a conversation growing out of the same afternoon's events, and having a bearing upon the same looked-for results. The latter had seemed to be in deeper thought even than usual for some time after Colonel White and Lucy left, and maintained a perfect silence except when spoken to by his mother. But after their frugal supper was over, he said, —

"Mother, did Colonel White give you anything for what I did for him this afternoon?"

"Yes, he did. He said you told him he might pay me."

"How much did he give you, mother?"

"A ten-dollar bill."

"What! ten dollars?"

"Yes, my son."

"Mother, I only meant for you to take pay for my riding his young horse home, and bringing back the other; but he has paid you that large amount because he thinks I saved him and his little girl from being hurt — perhaps from being killed. I wish you hadn't taken it; I don't feel right about it."

Mrs. Herrick, however, placed the matter before her son in the same light that the colonel had presented it to her, which had the effect to do away with his objections in a great measure.

"Colonel White seemed to think that you might feel somewhat as you do about the money, and so he took pains to give his views on the subject."

"The colonel is a first-rate man," said the boy, with emphasis. "I'm glad he explained the thing as he did, for I could never think of taking money for saving anybody's life."

"Yes, Colonel White is a most excellent man," replied Mrs. Herrick, with a grateful tone. "You don't know what he offers to do for us."

"What is it, mother?"

She now proceeded to lay the whole matter before George, arguing strongly in favor of the colonel's proposition as she went along. When she had finished, she was surprised, and sadly disappointed, at the reception the kind gentleman's offer met with, as her son merely said, —

" Colonel White is very good."

The poor woman looked in mute astonishment, as the boy leaned his head in silence upon the table. Neither of them spoke for some minutes. George finally broke the spell by a change of subject.

" When did you hear anything from *California*, mother?" The peculiar tone of voice, and the emphasis, plainly indicated that he had purposely substituted a geographical name for that of an individual.

" Not for a long, long time, my son."

" Do you ever expect to hear anything?"

" I cannot say that I do."

George sprang suddenly to his feet and walked to the window, keeping his back towards his mother, who looked anxiously after him during another painful silence. At length she crossed the room to where he stood, and, kissing his forehead, said, tremblingly, —

" My dear boy, what *is* the matter?"

He put his arm lovingly around his mother's waist, walked back with her to the table, gently pushed her into a chair, and seated himself before her. He then said, very deliberately, —

" Mother, I must talk to you about *him*, or I shall die."

" Well, my dear child, talk."

" Mother, I have suffered more in my mind for the last year than I can tell. I have had all sorts of thoughts — some very wicked ones, I know. Sometimes I have felt as if I could kill *him*, almost. Then again, once, when I was up to the trout-brook alone, fishing, I thought about drowning *myself;* but I knew that was *cowardly*, as well as wicked, and so I thought no more about it. But still, I have been feeling worse and worse about *him*. I know *he* left you, my dear mother, to take care of yourself and me, year after year, without coming or sending to see how you got along, and the thought has been more than I could bear. And then to think that *you* must love such a man, and that *I* must *try* to respect him! Mother, I can't — I *can't!* O, I wish he was not my father!" and the poor excited boy buried his face in his mother's lap.

" And so, my dear, dear son, you have been suffering all this for a long time, and yet kept it to yourself?" said Mrs. Herrick, as the tears flowed down her cheeks.

" Yes, mother; I thought that if you loved and respected *him*, I should only make you unhappier by saying anything. And I have hoped that *you* would say something to *me* about it."

" My dear, kind boy! I ought to have said

something to you about it, and certainly should have
done so if I had mistrusted for a moment that you
were thinking of it.   I have always intended to inform·
you of certain events that transpired before your recollection, but thought I would wait till I was sure you
could understand the matter fully.   I am convinced
now, however, that I should have confided all to you
long since."

"Let me know everything now, my dear mother."

"I will.   It is a long story, and a portion of it
humiliating, perhaps; but now is the time for you to
hear it."

"You can trust me, mother."

"You already know," began Mrs. Herrick, "that,
although this town is my native place, I have not
always lived here.   When I was fourteen years of age
I went to live with my only sister, who was married,
and resided in New York city.   When I was about
sixteen, I became acquainted with two young men,
cousins, George and James Herrick.   One of them
was master of a fine packet ship running between
New York and New Orleans, and the other was first
mate of the same vessel.   They were intimate friends
of Mr. Gregory, my sister's husband, and were at the
house nearly every evening when in port.   They
were very gentlemanly, and both showed me a good

deal of attention. My preference, however, was for the captain, who soon offered himself to me, was accepted, and before I was seventeen we were married.

"My husband hired and furnished a small, genteel house near my sister's, and we commenced house-keeping. He was all kindness to me, and there was no drawback to our happiness except on account of his absence a great part of the time, occasioned by his business. When I had been married short of a year, and during the absence of my husband, my sister suddenly died of heart disease. This was a severe blow to me, and I now felt very lonely. When Captain Herrick arrived, he was easily persuaded by me to give up his ship to his cousin James, for the present at least, and remain at home. He soon engaged in business to his mind, and we were very happy. His business was profitable, he appeared satisfied with it, and I hoped he would conclude to give up altogether going to sea. And when you were born, my son, it seemed as if my cup of happiness was full.

"Soon, however, I was brought to grief. Your father's health began rapidly to fail, and his physician pronounced him to be in a quick consumption. Alas! it was too true; before you were a year old, *your father was no more.*"

George Herrick again sprang to his feet with a

5

suddenness that came near overturning the table at his side, and exclaimed, almost wildly, —

"Mother, what is this you say?—what do I hear?—am *I* crazy? or are *you?* My father died when I was a year old! What do you mean? Mother, mother! won't you explain?" and the boy, in his bewilderment, walked rapidly up and down the little room.

"Yes, yes, my son, I will explain all; only be calm."

George took his seat again.

"I will *try* to be calm, mother. But you say such strange things!"

Mrs. Herrick continued: —

"Captain *George* Herrick was your father, my dear boy — Captain *James* Herrick is my second husband —".

"I see — I see — I understand. Then that man who deserted you and went to California is not my father? But say it again, mother! Speak it once more — do!"

"No, my son, he is *not* your father."

"Thank Heaven! Thank Heaven for that!" fervently exclaimed the excited boy. "Bless you, mother, for those words! I feel as if I could look *anybody* in the face now. I have felt so bitter, so *very* bitter against that man! And it is *such* a happiness to know that I have not felt so towards *my father!* But I don't understand it all yet, mother."

" I suppose not; but you will when you have heard all. I cannot finish the painful story to-night, however. We are both too much excited; we will be calmer in the morning, and then you shall hear the rest."

CHAPTER VIII.

GEORGE MAKES A PROMISE.

WO or three weeks before your father's death,"
continued Mrs. Herrick, " his cousin James
arrived at New York, and, on learning how
sick he was, at once requested the owners of the ship
to put some one else in command for that voyage, as
he wished to devote his time to his sick friend. He
was at our house every day, frequently remained all
night, taking full charge of your father, so as to
relieve me of the fatigue as much as possible; and in
every way seemed to be a true friend to me in my
trouble.

" After your father's death, Captain Herrick advised
me as to the best method of proceeding to secure the
property which had been left me (something like
fifteen thousand dollars), so that it would be as little
trouble to me as possible. In fact, he took full charge
of the whole matter, and thus relieved me of all the
care. I thought it would be best for me to sell off my

furniture, and return home here to Harryseekit, and live with father and mother at the old homestead. He informed me, however, that some of your father's business could not be settled up advantageously short of a year, and that I had better remain in New York till that was done. So I sold my furniture, and went to board in a nice family where I was acquainted. Mr. Gregory seemed to forget all about me after my sister's death, and took no interest in my affairs.

" Captain Herrick resumed command of his vessel when she returned to New York, but always called upon me when in the city, was very kind and thoughtful, and brought you many little presents.

" I mourned your father's death deeply and sincerely. But more affliction was in store for me. When I had been a widow a little less than a year, I received the painful intelligence that my father and mother had both been drowned by the upsetting of a sail-boat, during a squall in the bay, being on their way home from one of the islands, where they had been visiting a friend. I was now truly alone in the world, with the exception of you, my darling babe.

" I was the only heir to my father's property here, and of course it was necessary for me to do something about it. Captain Herrick was absent when I received the news ; but as soon as he arrived, and called to see

me, I made known to him the circumstances, and
asked his advice. He at once said that he had come
to see me for the express purpose of begging me to
confer upon him the right of being my adviser, not
only at that time, but through life, by becoming his
wife.

" I was very much surprised, and at first uttered a
refusal. He warmly avowed, however, that he had
always loved me ; but as his cousin had declared *his*
love first, and was accepted, he had buried his great
disappointment in his own bosom. But now, as he
had allowed me to mourn my loss a year, as I was
young, with a young child, and no relative to advise or
protect me, he had come, he said, in all truth and
honor, to offer me his heart and hand.

" My son, I did wrong, for my heart still clung to
the memory of your dead father ; but still, under the
circumstances, perhaps it is not surprising that I accepted his proposal, for I considered him an honorable
gentleman, and my devoted friend. We were married
at once. I placed the fullest confidence in him, of
course, or I should not have married him. He re-
signed the command of his ship, and set to work
immediately to arrange our affairs so that we could
come to Harryseekit and look after the property left
by my father. He informed me that his own funds

(ten thousand dollars) were invested in New York bank stock, which he considered the safest and best investment, and advised me to let him make the same disposition of mine. I consented to the arrangement, feeling that he knew all about such matters, and believing that he would do whatever was best for us all.

" As soon as this arrangement was made, we came to Harryseckit, and took possession of the old homestead — the place where Mr. Sinclair now lives. So far I had received nothing but the tenderest care from him, and he was very kind to you. We had been here only a few weeks, when he said to me that Mr. Sinclair wanted to buy the place, and had offered several hundred dollars more than it was really worth, and he thought we had better sell, and go back to New York, as he did not feel very well contented here: I agreed to it, thinking it my duty.

" The bargain was closed at once, and the money all paid down, amounting to two thousand three hundred dollars, with the stipulation that we could, if we chose, remain in the house three months, thus giving us ample time to make arrangements for removing to New York. Captain Herrick passed the three hundred dollars over to me, to meet incidental expenses, he said, and in a day or two left for New York to

invest the two thousand, and to make arrangements
for our change of residence.

"He was absent four weeks, and wrote to me but
once. My heart began to fail me. I feared that all
was not right. On the very day that he returned I
noticed a marked change in his behavior. He found
fault with me, about various little matters, for the
first time, and was extremely cross to you. I was
wretched. The next day he informed me that he
had changed his mind about going to New York. I
asked him why, and he said, *because he had*. I began
to fear that he had married me for the property I possessed; but still I could not believe it. A day or two
after this, while he was at the Corner, I entered his
room for something, and saw a letter lying on the floor.
I picked it up. It was a letter he had received when
last in New York from a man in Boston. I cast my
eye over it, and these words struck my notice : ' I *was*
greatly surprised, as you thought I might be, on hearing that you had married a widow with a *little encum-
brance ;* but, of course, the *fifteen thousand* makes all
the difference imaginable ; and, as you say, California
is a convenient place for *settling family difficulties.*' I
remained stupefied for an hour.

"But why continue this sad tale? In a day or two
he left for California, saying he would remit me

money; but of course I placed no confidence in what he said. I wrote to a friend in New York to inquire about the bank stock; and, as I expected, found that he had sold all, and pocketed the funds.

"I found a purse in my bureau drawer, after he left, containing a hundred dollars. With that and what I had left of the three hundred I purchased this little place to shelter you and me, my son, and had about fifty dollars remaining. My long, sad story is finished."

"My dear mother," exclaimed George, as he threw both arms around her neck, "I wonder how you have lived through all this! But now tell me, O, tell me, do you still love that cruel man who deceived and robbed you?"

"I cannot say that I do."

"Then promise me, if he ever comes back, that you will not live with him."

"I promise."

"Now, dear mother, I will make *my* promise, for I have work to do, and I mean to do it. I accept Colonel White's kind offer, and I will profit by it too. I will waste no more time. And, if I live, *you shall never need any one to provide for you or protect you.*"

"I do not doubt it, my son. I have all confidence in you. But wait a moment."

Mrs. Herrick stepped into her little bedroom, and returned in a moment or two with a daguerrotype, which she placed in George's hand, saying, —

"That, my son, is the picture of your father. I have kept it for *you;* *I* have forfeited my right to it. I can only say to you, respect his memory through life, and profit by his example, for he was a man of uniform kindness, and unwavering truth and honor — in a word, he was a sincere and consistent Christian."

"Mother, I think I can promise that I will. And although I know that what you have told me about yourself has made you feel very unhappy, and some parts of it have made me feel so too, yet now that I know that that wicked man who has deceived and robbed you is not my father, and that I shall not have to try any longer to respect him, I feel as if I could hold up my head among folks. Mother, you needn't be ashamed of me any more."

"I have never been ashamed of you, my son; but I have been worried about you because you have seemed to be unhappy."

"Well, all shall be right now. I'll go and see our friend, Colonel White, right off, and tell him we accept his offer."

"The sooner the better, my boy."

And he did go, and was received with a hearty welcome by the colonel and his wife ; and the result was, that within a fortnight, Mrs. Herrick and George were snugly domiciled with Uncle Bill and his wife, Aunt Betsey, and were fully under the fatherly care of Colonel White. In this comfortable situation they are found by the reader three years later, — the period at which our story commences, — the intervening time having been marked by great advantage to George Herrick, and perfect satisfaction resting with all the parties concerned.

CHAPTER IX.

WAR MEETING.

HE Monday after the reception of the news of the surrender of Fort Sumter on Saturday, was a stirring time in Harryscekit, as it was, indeed, throughout the length and breadth of all the free states. It seemed as if one grand pulsation moved every loyal heart, and sent thrills of patriotic fire through the swelling arteries of a nation of freemen.

Men and boys were fast assembling at the Corner, at an early hour in the morning, and many were ready to enlist on the moment; but as yet there seemed to be no order or system adopted. Several recommendations had been made, but nothing was done. Directly Colonel White made his appearance among them, when all turned to him for some suggestion.

" The first thing to be done, in my opinion," said that gentleman, " is to call a meeting in the Town Hall at the earliest possible hour, and decide upon some plan of action. We shall, without doubt, hear

from the governor and adjutant-general by one or two
o'clock to-day ; but there is not a moment to lose, and
we can do much in the mean time. All that is wanted
is concert of action."

This suggestion met the approval of all; and the
colonel and one or two others immediately called on
Mr. Clark, chairman of the selectmen of the town,
who lived near by, and pressed the matter upon him.
He at once instructed the clerk to notify the citizens
that there would be a war meeting in the Town Hall
at twelve o'clock that day. Colonel White urged the
propriety of giving thorough notice throughout the
town, so that all sections might be represented, and
all have an equal opportunity to respond to this first
call for volunteers. He said he would furnish his
horse and buggy, with a driver, to take the notices to
a remote part of the town in one direction, and by
starting off messengers in other directions in a similar
manner, they could notify in season nearly every man
in the place. The plan was adopted. And George
Herrick and Tom Sprightly, seated behind Dancing
Jim in Colonel White's buggy, had the honor and the
satisfaction of notifying the inhabitants of one portion
of the town to the first war meeting in Harryseekit.

Our two young friends were in high spirits. This
early opportunity that the colonel had given them to

work in their country's cause seemed an earnest to
them that their old friend would fulfil his promise of
the previous Saturday evening, and continue to point
out their duties in the same line. Although they
thought their present occupation rather tame, to what
it would be to march boldly forth to meet the rebels on
the battle-field, still they were determined to perform
their home duties well. George Herrick was far too
thoughtful a boy, and placed too much confidence in
his patron's good judgment and friendship, to brood
long over any disappointment; and Tom Sprightly's
spirits, being as elastic as his limbs, if they did not
perform as many somersets, were never depressed for
any great length of time. Consequently both boys
were quite well satisfied with their present employment, and with their expectations for the future.

Tom's legs, whose running qualities have been
hinted at before, did excellent service, in the present
instance, by carrying notices of the meeting to several
houses situated at considerable distances from the main
road, and then he would run across fields and pastures
to intercept George and the buggy at some point
farther on — thus saving much time. They left a
message at every house on their route, and were the
first to report progress at the Corner, where they were
complimented for their despatch.

As we gave Dancing Jim a bad name on a former occasion, it will be doing him no more than justice to say here, that his conduct for the last year or two had been unexceptionable. He still retained the name given him by Mrs. White, but his *dancing* days were over. He was perfectly steady at all times; and the colonel had the pleasure of taking frequent drives with his wife by his side, who now had no occasion for the slightest fear. Whether this change had been brought about by the good examples of his old fellow-horse, or through his own instincts of what the duties of a well-treated horse might be, or whether it was to be attributed to the good training he had received at the hands of George Herrick,—under whose especial charge he was placed for a whole year immediately after his dangerous freak with Colonel White and Lucy,—we leave the reader to decide according to the evidence in the case.

The result of this extra exertion made by a few of the energetic citizens of Harryseekit was, that by half past twelve o'clock there was a larger gathering at the Town Hall than had been seen there for many years. The meeting was called to order and organized, and the chairman briefly stated its object. Colonel White at once moved that a company roll be prepared for volunteers to sign, and that a subscription paper be placed on the table for such sums as individuals might see fit to give for the purpose of assisting any volunteers who might need ready money, or for the help of their families during their absence. The motion was seconded, and declared open for discussion.

Several speakers addressed the meeting briefly, all in favor of the motion ; some declaring their readiness to enroll their names as soon as the roll was ready, while others offered to subscribe liberal sums on the other paper. Many, however, in urging the matter forward, spoke of the probable briefness of the coming struggle, even if there were to be any fighting at all, seeming to think that the Southerners would recede as soon as they became aware of the firm stand taken by the government and by the whole loyal people. One speaker went so far as to say that undoubtedly many very young men — from sixteen to eighteen years of age — would be anxious to enlist, and he thought they might be safely taken, as there would probably be but one campaign, and that a short one, and this class could be spared from home much better than older men. He also thought that the call of the president for seventy-five thousand men was in excess of the real demands of the case. However, he was in favor of raising them.

There was quite a crowd of lads present, ranging

from fifteen to eighteen years of age, including Tom and George, interested listeners to the proceedings of this stirring meeting. When the speaker alluded to the younger class of patriots, he was greeted with applause from their quarter of the house — thus receiving evidence that he had not miscalculated on their willingness to enlist.

Colonel White now took the floor. Every sound was hushed, for he was always listened to with much deference when he addressed a meeting of any description, and, in the present instance, his remarks were looked forward to with more than usual interest, on account of his experience in military matters. He commenced by saying that he was much gratified at the unanimity of opinion expressed as to the furtherance of the main object of the meeting — that of raising men and money to meet the pressing urgency of the case. He regretted, however, to be obliged to differ from some of the speakers on minor points.

"In the first place," continued the colonel, "with reference to the president's call for men. One gentletleman thinks a less number of volunteers than are called for would have answered the demands of the case. But, Mr. Chairman, I wish the president had asked for two hundred thousand instead of seventy-five thousand. I have no wish to magnify the coming

6

danger; but, my friends, more men, many more, will
be needed. Just consider, for a moment, the extent
of the line that will have to be marked by the border
states. We cannot say with any certainty at the
present time where that border will be; but, wherever
it proves to be, its extent will reach thousands of miles,
and its entire length will have to be' almost one continued palisade of bristling bayonets. Hence it is easy
to see that seventy-five thousand men cannot possibly
be in excess of the demand.

" But it will be said that this argument rests upon
the ground that the South is to maintain the stand
she has taken, and that a general civil war will be
the result; which some of the speakers here to-day
think will not be the case. But, fellow-citizens, let
me tell you that the ambitious, wicked men at the
South, who are forcing the masses of their people into
this most uncalled-for rebellion, would never have
attempted this high-handed assault upon our government had they not believed themselves well prepared
to follow it up; and now, having gone thus far, they
cannot recede. The brand of traitor is stamped on
their foreheads, and their doom is sealed, unless they
succeed in their treasonable . designs. They have
staked their all on this diabolical stroke, and are
determined to rule or die. And as they have been

preparing whilst we have been sleeping, and as they are a brave people as well as we, they must naturally gain some advantages during our period of preparation, and thus be encouraged to make still greater exertion. And, fellow-citizens, though I have not the glimmer of a doubt but that our government will, eventually, crush this wicked rebellion totally and forever, giving new splendor to our free institutions, and additional strength to our blessed Union, yet, before this is done, armies are to be marshalled and battles are to be fought on such a scale of immensity as the world never yet dreamed of. I say not this to discourage, but to stimulate. We must realize the imminence of the danger in order to prepare for it.

" A few words more, Mr. Chairman, and I will close. One gentleman has alluded to our *boys,* and to their undoubted willingness to enlist, and spoken of their ability to meet the requirements of a soldier's life. Of their willingness to serve their country I have not the slightest doubt; for at an early hour Saturday evening, two of our village lads, neither of them much over fifteen years of age, called upon me for advice on this very matter, having made up their minds, on the first reception of the news of the fall of Fort Sumter, to enlist at once, and wanted to take the first train this morning for Boston, and join some regiment there, in order to be among the first volunteers to arrive at Washington."

This statement was responded to by cheers from all parts of the house.

"But," continued the old gentleman, "I advised them — as I do now every young man within the sound of my voice who is under eighteen — *not* to enlist at present. Fellow-citizens, I had an opportunity to see the folly, the *wickedness*, of having boys or very young men in the army during that disastrous campaign of 1813 on the northern frontier, intended to capture Montreal, in which the young, brave, and energetic General Brown rescued our army from the perilous situation in which it had been placed by the incompetency, or something worse, of Generals Wilkinson and Hampton. At one time during the winter, nearly one half of the army was down from fatigue and exposure ; and that half contained *about all* of the younger portion.

"Mr. Chairman, and friends, I entreat you not to send your *boys* into the army when it is not absolutely necessary, for it is misery to them, and of no benefit to government ; but let us set good examples before them here at home, and cause their love of country to strengthen with their growth, so that they may here-after be of real value in the Union ranks if they are needed. In the mean time there will be work enough here, and patriotic work, too, for them to do. And there will be opportunity for us old men to do something for the good cause also; ay, and our wives and daughters likewise can lend important help. Fellow-citizens, let us remember this one thing as all-important — that however much our success in this war may depend upon the endurance and the bravery of our soldiers on the field, nearly, if not equally, as much depends upon our unremitting exertions and *patriotism at home.*"

As Colonel White took his seat, a round of applause burst forth from all parts of the hall, his remarks having met with the hearty approval of all present; even some of those who had taken different views of the matter at an earlier stage of the meeting being the first to acknowledge that the colonel had the right of the case.

Squire Belmont, a wealthy citizen, who had headed the subscription list with two hundred dollars, and had been followed by Colonel White with the like amount, now rose, and said he would like to ask the last speaker for the names of the two lads who had thus early signified to him their readiness to enlist. The colonel replied by giving the names — George Herrick and Thomas Sprightly. The announcement was greeted with loud applause. Squire Belmont then said, —

" I shall always consider these two boys as the first volunteers from Harryseekit, and I propose three cheers for them."

The cheers were given with a will.

Colonel White again took the floor, and said, —

" Mr. Chairman, pardon me for one moment more. I merely wish to take this opportunity to pledge my word to the boys of Harryseekit, that if they will meet at my house once a week, I will use what military knowledge I possess in giving them instructions until they become well acquainted with company drill."

Three enthusiastic cheers were now given for Colonel White. The motion offered by that gentleman at the opening of the meeting was then passed unanimously, the selectmen were constituted a finance committee to take charge of the funds raised, and to pay them over to the proper persons, and the meeting adjourned.

During the progress of the meeting the expected order had been received from the adjutant-general calling upon all volunteers, in companies, to report to him at the State House at the earliest moment, and receive their arms and equipments. And the patriotic people of Harryseckit had the satisfaction of seeing a company of one hundred true and hardy men leave their railroad depot that evening by the ten o'clock train for the capital of the state, where they formed a part of the first regiment that left that point for the defence of Washington.

Directly after the adjournment of the meeting at the Town Hall, the boys assembled on the green in front of the building, and decided to accept Colonel White's offer to drill them. All the boys were considerably excited, and Tom Sprightly was particularly lavish with his " peppermint and shoestrings," and offered to turn " to order " any number of somersets that might be demanded.

The boys finally dispersed, with the determination to consult their parents with regard to the scheme of forming a company.

CHAPTER X.

TOM SPRIGHTLY AND BOOBY CHICKENS.

AS Tom was somewhat of a favorite with the boys of Harryseekit, the reader may as well consider him in the play, and endeavor to overlook some of his wild pranks in consideration of any commendable qualities that may show forth through his frolicsome nature. Perhaps it is not wholly impossible that his particular friend, George Herrick, may ultimately have as good success in taming *him*, as he has already displayed in improving the behavior of Colonel White's wild colt.

That a warm friendship existed between these two boys, notwithstanding the great dissimilarity in their temperaments, actions, and conversation, the reader, of course, has ere this discovered. There were a number of good reasons for this friendship. When George first came into that neighborhood, and entered school, although a bright, intelligent boy, — as he has shown himself to be from the first, — he was behindhand in his studies. Now, Tom was a bright scholar. He could understand a principle at a glance, and possessed a very retentive memory. Notwithstanding he seemed scarcely to study his lessons at all, yet he never failed. He could commit page after page to memory by merely reading the matter over once or twice.

He at once volunteered to assist George Herrick in his lessons, as soon as he saw how matters stood, and this enabled him soon to become one of the first scholars in the school. George appreciated this kindness. Tom, although he made use of many foolish expressions, was never profane. This corresponded with George's principles and practice. Then, again, the former, although he would utter most extravagant assertions for the sake of fun and frolic (which we do not pretend to excuse in him), might safely be depended upon as strictly a boy of truth in any matter of importance. This, also, met the entire approbation of the latter, who utterly despised a falsehood.

George, on his part, had given his volatile young friend much good advice at different times, for which Tom was, in reality, truly thankful, though in most cases he was sure to turn the matter into a joke at the time. Finally, as already briefly alluded to by Tom, George had, on one occasion, saved him from serious injury, if not from death, by rescuing him from a furious animal.

Tom had, on the occasion alluded to, jumped over the fence into Squire Belmont's pasture, and commenced bellowing, and throwing up dirt in the face and eyes of a savage bull owned by that gentleman, trusting to his own nimbleness of foot to get out of the way when he should have sufficiently attracted the animal's ire. The bull soon rushed at the foolish boy, and he sprang to the fence; but some part of his clothing caught on a knot, and the furious brute dashed madly upon him. Fortunately his horns missed him. As the creature drew back for a second attack, George Herrick sprang over the fence and dealt him such heavy blows on his nose and fore legs with a heavy club, as caused him to beat a retreat long enough for the two boys to put the fence between them and danger.

George had endeavored to persuade Tom from the foolish adventure; but he laughed at the advice, and came near paying dearly for his temerity. We have the promise in his own words, that for this timely assistance he would "stand by George Herrick as long as he lived."

Tom Sprightly was a favorite with the boys generally because he was always good-natured, all life and spirits, full of jokes, puns, conundrums, odd sayings, and fun of almost every description, being able to string off any amount of rhyming nonsense, *impromptu*, which, though devoid of anything like poetry, generally contained sufficient wit to please his mates; so there was sure to be sport of some sort whenever he was present.

He has feelingly alluded to his mother, who had been dead about two years, thus showing that there was true filial affection in his heart. His father died before Tom's recollection, and since his mother's death his home had been with his aunt Huldah French, his mother's sister.

Mrs. French was a clever, warm-hearted woman, indulgent to her children, and kind and obliging to her neighbors. She had always treated Tom equally as well as her own children, though she sometimes attempted to scold him for some of his pranks; but Tom invariably managed on such occasions to hug, and kiss, and joke his aunt into positive good nature, and usually wound up the skirmish by insisting on "titillating his olfactory nerves" with a fine, brown powder, which the good woman carried very choicely and somewhat slyly in a neat little box in her pocket, — which operation the impudent young fellow called "*snuffing* the pipe of peace."

Mr. French was a good-natured, easy sort of a man,

carrying on the cabinet-making business at the village.
He employed a few men, paid all his bills as he went
along, and made a comfortable living; and this seemed
to give him perfect satisfaction. He was fully as indulgent as his wife to our friend Tom, and consequently that youth had a very easy time of it. True,
for the last year he had been an apprentice in his
uncle's shop; but he was as quick at his work as he
had been at his studies, and as Mr. French usually
gave him a certain amount of work to do each day as
a stint, through his expertness and ingenuity Tom
managed to have about half his time to himself;
though — to his credit be it said — he always performed his task promptly and thoroughly.

The cabinet-maker had recently obtained the nick-
name " *Booby French;* " not that he was, by any
means, dull or stupid, but " Booby " had been coupled
with his name through a ludicrous little incident, which
we will here relate.

A Mr. Melcher, living at a distant part of the town,
had come into possession of a few fowls of a large and
improved breed, called " *booby hens,*" and he kindly
furnished Mr. French with a dozen of the eggs, which
he placed under one of his own setting hens in order
to obtain a flock of " boobies."

Now, Tom said he thought all hens were big

"boobies," for you might put any kind of eggs under them, and they would hatch them all the same, and never know the difference. For his part, he didn't think it was right to play such tricks on a poor, ignorant hen! Mr. French, however, had no scruples of the kind, and had told all his neighbors that he was expecting a brood of "booby" chickens, and promised to furnish them all with "booby" eggs next season.

As no chickens appeared at the usual time, the conclusion was, that "booby" eggs had *very thick shells.* At the close of another week, however, Madam Biddy stalked forth, much delighted, with ten little "boobies." Mr. French and his wife were nearly as much pleased as the hen herself; but Tom was apparently more delighted than any of the party.

"Peppermint and shoestrings!" he exclaimed; "if this old hen don't take first-rate care of these little 'boobies,' she deserves to be well *ducked.*"

After a day or two, Tom's aunt said to Mr. French, —

"Husband, those are the queerest-looking chickens I ever saw. They look more like ducklings than anything else."

So the whole family went out to look at them.

"They do look a *little* like ducks," replied Mr. French; "but then they will change their appearance very much as soon as they begin to feather out."

"If they don't improve fast enough," said Tom, very soberly, "aunt Huldah can give them a little of her *quack* medicine."

"You'd better not make fun of my medicine, Tom," replied his aunt, not knowing that his witticism was intended to cut in two directions; "you are glad enough to take some of it yourself when you have a bad cold."

"So I am," responded Tom. "But these are rather queer-looking chicks, any way. I wish I could think who it was that said that young "boobies" always looked like ducks!"—but Tom *couldn't* think.

The next day Mr. French invited some of his neighbors in to see his family of chickens. They were growing nicely, and the visitors congratulated Mrs. French on having such a fine brood of "boobies;" but all remarked, "How much they look like ducks!"

A day or two later, Tom rushed into the house, exclaiming,—

"Aunt Huldah, you'll certainly have to put some of your ' Composition' to steep for your 'boobies,' for that fool of an old hen has contrived to get them all into the mud puddle out here, and they'll surely take their death of cold."

"Don't bother me with your nonsense now, Tom; I'm in a hurry," replied Mrs. French, continuing at her work.

"There's no nonsense about it, aunt, unless it's the nonsense of that old hen herself; she don't know how to take care of those little darling 'boobies' half as well as an old waddling duck would. I tell you, truly, they're all in the water."

Now, Mrs. French knew Tom well enough to understand that he really meant what he said in this last sentence; so she at once left her work, and followed him to the door.

"I *do* declare! if that don't beat *me!*" she exclaimed, holding up both hands; for, true enough, there were all her little "boobies" swimming about in the muddy water, bobbing their tiny heads underneath it, and seeming to have a good time generally; while the bewildered old hen was racing around the edge of the puddle, clucking, and screeching, and making all the noises that a terrified hen-mother is capable of.

At this moment Mr. French came into the yard, and burst forth into a loud, merry laugh as he looked at the ludicrous picture—his wife standing in amazement with uplifted hands, Tom half-knee deep in the muddy water, apparently endeavoring to catch the aquatic sporters, which were scudding about in every direction, while the old hen was racing and squalling around the margin of the little pond in the greatest possible distress.

"What kind of a show have you here, wife?" he asked, as he reached her side.

"Really, I don't know," she replied; "I almost begin to think there is some witchcraft about this hen and her chickens."

"I think you had better send this old hen and her queer brood, mud puddle and all, to Barnum, and let him put the whole thing into his Aquatic Garden," suggested Tom to his uncle.

"These things look and act more and more like ducks every day," said Mr. French. "I don't know what to make of it. Melcher didn't say a word about their looking like ducks, or going into the water. And he said the eggs were the real 'English boobies.'"

"I guess he made one mistake," replied Tom. "I'll bet a pinch of aunt Huldah's snuff that they were *French* 'boobies,' and that's the reason the hen and chickens can't understand each other."

"Well," responded his uncle, "Melcher will probably be down to the Corner again in a day or two, and I'll get him to look in and see if he can understand it. I have no doubt but they will come out all right at last."

"They are coming out *now*," said Tom, as the whole brood began to scramble up on one side of the little puddle, much to the joy of the old hen.

During the next few days Mrs. French had more callers than she could well attend to, and all must see the "booby" chickens. They were much admired; but still came the exclamation, "How much they look like ducks!"

Whenever Tom was present, he explained, that there was a large water-fowl, of the pelican tribe, called the "*booby;*" and probably this name had been given to this kind of hen because the chickens, when quite young, had an inclination to take to the water, and also because they *slightly* resembled the duck.

The question was finally settled, however, by Mr. Melcher himself, whom Mr. French brought home with him one day. The moment that gentleman saw the hen and her brood, he exclaimed, —

"Why, French, these things were never hatched from the eggs I brought you — they are *nothing but ducks!*"

Mr. French looked at his wife, his wife looked at Mr. French, they both looked at Mr. Melcher, all looked at Tom; and Tom looked at the old hen and her ducks for a moment, and then cried out, with apparent indignation, —

7

"Peppermint and shoestrings! this is too bad! but I told you, uncle French, at the commencement, that all hens were 'boobies;' that you could never tell what they would hatch out, and that they never knew themselves what they had hatched. I really believe if you had put a lot of frog's eggs under that old hen, she would have hatched them all out, and expected them *to crow!*"

"O, Tom, Tom," exclaimed Mrs. French, while all three were heartily laughing at his odd conceit, "this is some of your work, and I don't know as I shall ever forgive you. Mr. Melcher took so much pains to bring us those eggs, and then to have you throw them away for a lot of duck's eggs!"

"Aunt Huldah," expostulated Tom, "how can you think I would do such a thing as throw away a dozen eggs — especially 'booby' eggs? I shouldn't expect you to forgive me if I had done such a thing. But I don't see how I'm to blame for their turning to duck's eggs."

"That won't do, Tom; I *know* this must be some of your work," repeated his aunt.

"Mr. Melcher," said Tom, turning to that gentleman, "I would like to have you come now and see *my* boobies; I've got some of the pure breed — some of the regular school — no *quackery* about mine;" and

Tom led the way round the end of the wood-shed, where, sure enough, was another hen, with a full dozen of as bright-looking chickens as one would wish to see.

" What do you think of those, Mr. Melcher?" asked Tom, pointing with pride to the brood of little chirpers. " *My* 'booby' eggs didn't turn to duck's eggs, and come out web-footed."

Mr. Melcher at once pronounced Tom's flock of chickens to be of the genuine " booby" breed.

" Now, aunt Huldah," said Tom, " notwithstanding you accused me of throwing away your eggs, I'll do the fair thing by you. I'll give you these twelve real 'boobies' for your ten little flat-bills, and you must give me a pinch of snuff to boot."

" Agreed," replied his aunt, laughing. " And now, Tom, tell us how it all happened."

" What! tell you how ducks were hatched from hen's eggs? Why should I know how it's done? That *lays* with the old hen, and she must *set* it right; " and Tom turned a somerset, and away he ran down to the shop to relate the *finale* of the " booby" enterprise, leaving his uncle and aunt, with Mr. Melcher, to guess the matter out.

Not intending to leave the reader guessing, however, we will merely say that the next day after the "booby" eggs were put under the hen, Tom found another hen preparing to set; so he procured a dozen duck's eggs and substituted them for the "booby" eggs, and put the latter under the second hen. Consequently, about a week before the first hen came out with her ducks, the second marshalled forth her brood of genuine "boobies;" but as they varied very slightly at first from ordinary chickens, and as the first hen was the point of attraction to everybody but Tom, the ducks had received all the attention.

CHAPTER XI.

THE YOUNG INVINCIBLES.

OLONEL WHITE'S proposition to become the instructor of the boys in military tactics was so popular with them, that in the course of a few days they had a roll of fifty names — their ages ranging all the way from twelve to fifteen years. . George Herrick and Tom Sprightly took much interest in the movement, and, by consulting freely with the colonel, were enabled to give the other boys a good deal of information with regard to what was expected of them at first.

The greater part of them had the idea that they must have muskets to commence with ; and although many of the boys' parents were perfectly willing to furnish them, there were others that demurred, either because they thought the organization would amount to nothing, or from motives of economy. However, this difficulty was soon settled by word from Colonel White to the effect that he should drill them some time without arms or equipments, and then both they and their parents could judge better whether the object was of sufficient moment to warrant the trouble and expense of a military outfit. This arrangement suited the large majority of the boys, although some few, who had received the promise of a gun and equipments, felt a little disappointment at first, and thought there could not be much fun in being soldiers without arms.

While these youthful patriots of Harryseekit were discussing and making their little arrangements for the formation of their company, events were daily transpiring, in various parts of the country, that were the precursors of a mighty conflict of principles and of arms, which was to shake the government of this free people to its foundations, and startle Christendom with its magnitude and bloodshed. A few days after the surrender of Sumter came the news of the shooting of Massachusetts troops in Baltimore, followed closely by the burning of the Gosport Navy Yard, the secession of Virginia, loyal troops pouring into Washington by thousands, the stormy debates in Congress, the withdrawal of southern Congressmen, another call by President Lincoln for eighty-two thousand additional men for the army and navy, the capture of Alexandria and the murder of Colonel Ellsworth, the unfortunate battle at Great Bethel, where the gallant Major Winthrop lost his life, together with terrible threats and overt acts by the southern people generally.

All this, of course, served to fan the flame of patriotism that was burning in the breasts of all loyal people, and the boys of Harryseekit were not an exception. Probably some of these lads thought that the military movement they were about to engage in would afford them amusement and recreation merely; but the sequel will show whether any of them were prompted by motives of duty and love of country. At all events, by placing themselves under the instruction of so thorough a soldier, patriot, and Christian as was Colonel White, they were in a school where they could not fail to improve in some of the qualities that go to make up the honest and true citizen of a free Christian government.

Wednesday afternoon of each week was decided upon as drill-day, to accommodate such of the boys as attended school. At their first meeting, which took place on the green in front of Colonel White's house, ten days after the subject was first agitated, every boy whose name was enrolled was promptly on the ground at two o'clock, the appointed hour. The colonel had given George Herrick some private lessons in military tactics, as soon as he found that the boys seriously

entertained his proposition, in order that he might
have some little assistance if he deemed it necessary.
He now instructed him to form the boys into line,
according to size, and to say that he would be with
them in a few minutes. The boys were very orderly,
and George formed them in line with considerable
military precision. Colonel White presently made his
appearance, and addressed the company as follows : —

" Boys of Harryseekit : it gives me much satisfaction
to see you here so promptly and in such numbers, and,
above all, to see you so orderly; for *order* is the
one controlling element in all military operations, and
obedience to orders the first duty of a soldier. And
although I shall have neither the inclination nor the
authority to place you under guard for disobedience,
or *have you shot if you desert,* yet I trust and believe
that your conduct in the ranks will ever be such as
will redound to your own self-respect, to the honor of
your parents, and to the welfare of your beloved country, whose battles you may yet be called upon to
fight.

" Do not understand by this, my young friends, that
I intend to be a harsh disciplinarian with you : on the
contrary, I shall allow you much freedom of thought,
word, and action, especially while drilling you without
arms ; but I shall allow you this liberty by giving you

frequent 'rests' — at other times your own good sense will tell you that there must be no interruptions.

"I want you all to feel that you are really serving your country by this arrangement. All the importance of the matter does not consist in the mere fact that you will be gaining information in military tactics, thus fitting you, in a measure, for actual duty at some future day, should the country demand your services; but, if you conduct yourselves with propriety, your example will have its influence in other towns and states, and perhaps be the means of awakening the country to the importance of a general system of military instruction for the youth of the land.

"Finally, boys, as an organized company you will be much more efficient in performing patriotic duties here at home than you would otherwise be. And there will be no lack of opportunities for all of us to show our love of country. The helping hand of every man, woman, and child throughout the loyal states will be needed. And, boys of Harryseekit, I want each one of you to feel that it is to your willing hearts and strong hands in the future — and to those of your age throughout the land — that the government is to look for the completion of the work that our brave volunteers in the field are just now commencing. And I want each one of you to bear this important fact in mind, — as this deplorable strife progresses, and you hear different views expressed as to its cause and its continuance, — that the war was commenced by *a band of traitors firing on our glorious old flag*, and that it must never end so long as *one of those traitors continues in arms*."

The colonel's little speech was vociferously applauded by his attentive listeners, and Tom Sprightly remarked to his near companions, "I wish Colonel White could lead us right off to the seat of war, for I believe that any man or boy whose whole heart is in the cause, if he had to go on crutches, would be worth more than many an able-bodied, big two-fisted fellow who leaves his heart at home, and takes nothing but a *gizzard* with him."

"And a 'booby' gizzard at that, Tom," added Charlie Sprague at his side — the boy who had furnished Tom with some duck's eggs on a previous occasion.

Colonel White now proceeded to make a division of the company, finding the number too large for convenience. He placed twenty of them in one rank at such a distance from the others as to avoid any interference in the orders, and gave them in charge of George Herrick, giving his own attention to the larger portion placed in a similar manner. By taking his own position at a convenient distance in front of their centre, he concluded that he could command a better view of the whole than at any other point. George Herrick took a similar position in front of his squad, and the first lesson, which consisted of the " Position of the Soldier," commenced by the instructor and his assistant.

This lesson, the pupils were informed, was of great importance, and should be thoroughly learned, as it enabled the soldier always to occupy his allotted space and no more, to maintain an easy and graceful position, and to retain the full use of his limbs without interfering with his brother soldier to the right or left, front or rear. The colonel had a very easy and pleasing, but yet impressive way of imparting information, which rendered the task an agreeable one to the pupils ; and as George Herrick was almost idolized by the village boys, and fully understood this primary lesson, he was nearly as successful a teacher as the old gentleman himself.

Hence, in the course of an hour, these fifty boys, who had never given this subject the slightest attention before, made quite a military appearance, as far as position was concerned, standing with their heels in a perfectly straight line ; their feet forming the proper angle, and turned out with uniform precision ; their

knees were straight without stiffness, and their bodies
perpendicular, with a very slight forward inclination;
the shoulders properly thrown back, dropping equally,
with the arms hanging naturally, and the elbows close
to the sides; the face square to the front, but not in
a constrained manner, and the eyes directed to the
ground at some twelve or fifteen paces distant.

Colonel White occasionally passed over to George's
squad, pointing out any little irregularities that he
noticed, and making suggestions to the pupils, that
they might feel that they were really as much under
his instruction as the other rank was. He took particular pains to explain to the boys the utility of the
positions required, as well as their bearing on each
other, believing that any lesson makes a much deeper
impression upon the pupil if he knows the why and
the wherefore.

The colonel was highly gratified at the aptness of
his pupils, and complimented them for their attention
and progress; telling them, that notwithstanding these
first lessons might not interest them very much, still
they were of the utmost importance if they wished to
become thorough soldiers; and he presumed that each
successive lesson would prove more and more interesting to them.

The evidence, however, was good that this first

lesson in military instruction had not been uninterest-
ing to the boys; for when their instructor informed
them that they had been under drill for the space of
two hours, and that he should now dismiss them, they
were much surprised, and could scarcely believe that
so much time had elapsed.

Upon being dismissed, they gave three cheers for
Colonel White, and then collected around Uncle Bill,
who had stood looking over the fence at them during
the whole time they had been engaged.

"Well, Uncle Bill," said Tom Sprightly, turning a
somerset close to the old sailor's head, "what do you
think of our first attempt at military tactics?"

"O, you did very well for young land-lubbers,"
replied the old seaman, with a slight approach to a
smile at one corner of the mouth, and a quizzical wink
with one eye; "but you should have seen us 'boys in
blue' on the decks of 'Old Ironsides' under the
gallant Hull, if you wanted something good for sore
eyes."

"Did you ever want anything for *sore backs* on
board that delectable 'Old Ironsides,' Uncle Bill?"
asked Tom, with a knowing look.

"I don't recollect anything about that, you young
rogue," was the sober answer.

" Your memory don't extend *back* so far as that,"
suggested Tom.

" Come, now, Uncle Bill, candidly," said George
Herrick, " don't you think we did pretty well for
the first time? "

" Yes, yes, I suppose I may as well say that you
did," was the old sailor's answer, who was on most
excellent terms with all the lads of the village, though
it was a hard matter for him to admit that a boy could
be good for much on the land.

" Now, Uncle Bill," said Tom Sprightly, " we want
a name for our company, and as you have paid us the
first compliment, you shall have the honor of giving us
the name."

" Yes, a name! a name! " shouted a dozen boys in
the same breath.

" I don't know about that," replied the old sailor,
" for I haven't kept a very close reckoning in land
phrases, and I should probably find myself in the
wrong latitude."

" We'll risk that, Uncle Bill," said George Herrick;
" come, now for the name.   Attention — boys! "

" I'd ought to have a bottle to break, as we do at a
launching when the ship is named," suggested the old
seaman; and bringing his arm back suddenly as if in
the act of swinging the bottle, he struck Tom Sprightly

a slight blow in the mouth, which caused the youngster to spin around like a top, and exclaim; —

" Uncle Bill, I owe you one for that. Because you hadn't a bottle to break you thought you'd break my ' mug,' did you? "

Tom was not much hurt, and if he had been it would have passed for a good joke with him; so the boys all roared with laughter, and Uncle Bill asked his pardon. Then, swinging his hat in the air, the old sailor exclaimed, —

" Success to the *Young Invincibles !* "

" Good! good! " shouted Tom Sprightly; " three cheers for Uncle Bill and the name ! "

The cheers were heartily given. Colonel White, who had been standing a little one side enjoying the scene, now stepped forward among the merry group, and said, —

" Young Invincibles : our old friend here has given you a name that I trust will inspire you with a commendable ambition. Invincibility at home is of equal importance with that of the battle-field. You have only to prove yourselves, individually and collectively, *invincible to all wrong*, in order to stand forth with modest firmness as ever unvanquished."

The pupils and their instructor now separated, to meet again at the same hour and place a week hence.

The first drill of the Young Invincibles had thus proved perfectly satisfactory to all parties concerned, and their future meetings were looked forward to with much interest.

Our stanch old patriot, Colonel White, felt that there was a deeper importance attached to this work he had undertaken than all the military information he should be able to impart to his pupils, although he considered this of no slight moment. But he was one of the few who appeared to realize the magnitude and duration of the struggle that had already commenced, and he saw that the means, the patriotism, and the endurance of the people were to be taxed as never before since the Revolution. He knew there would be diverse opinions as to the measures of the government, and the management of the war; that there would be, as in all wars, conscientious peace men to meet with fair argument, and concealed and open traitors in our very midst to guard against and secure.

Anticipating all this, the patriotic old soldier concluded, that, in addition to what influence he might exert over his fellow-citizens generally, he could, at the same time he was imparting military information to the youth of the village, instil into their minds, or keep alive there, such a love of country as would have its effect upon every family so reached. Hence fifty warm-hearted and ardent boys were thus made to act as so many apostles of patriotism to keep alive the fire that might otherwise grow dim or expire. And thus would he be the means of adding to that *patriotism at home*, the influence of which he felt certain would be required to give support to our brave and hardy soldiers in the field. What nobler cause could an old soldier on the brink of the grave be engaged in? No wonder the boys all admired him!

8

CHAPTER XII.

NEIGHBORLY DUTIES.

COLONEL WHITE was not one of that class of men who forget or neglect the every-day duties of life in carrying out those which they consider of far greater importance. Hence, while he was himself earnestly engaged in acts of patriotism, and was urging upon his family and others the necessity of exerting themselves in the same direction, we still find him fully alive to those private, neighborly, Christian duties that are constantly arising in every social circle. He was particularly careful to caution the members of his own family against forgetting for a single day the demands upon them of the poor or the sick that had or might come to their knowledge.

The colonel did not content himself with forming a company of boys, but had also impressed Lucy with the idea of starting the project of an organization of young school-girls, to be called the " School-girls' Soldiers' Aid Society," whose labors should consist in

manufacturing little articles of comfort and convenience, and in collecting light sanitary stores, as well
as books, papers, or whatever might amuse or instruct,
and have the same forwarded at convenient seasons to
sick and wounded soldiers who would soon fill our hos-
pitals. Lucy commenced the work immediately, and
became very much interested in it; so much so, that
before many days she had a sufficient number enlisted
in the movement to form a society of quite a respectable size, and which her grandmother and some other
ladies immediately proceeded to organize in a proper
manner.

Colonel White, seeing that his granddaughter was
so much taken up with this movement, and fearing
that she might be forgetting some of her other duties,
said to her one evening, —

"Lucy, my darling, have you heard from Mrs.
Swift to-day?"

"O, yes, grandfather," she replied, in somewhat of
a surprised tone; "I never miss going there every
day. And George also calls every day or evening, to
see if there is anything he can do. But Lizzie says
that Tom Sprightly is so kind and attentive that he
scarcely leaves anything for the rest of the kind neighbors to do."

"I am very happy to hear that none of you have

forgotten that poor, suffering woman since this war excitement commenced. How was she to-day?"

"I don't see any change in her from day to day, and Lizzie says she don't, either; but by comparing her condition from month to month, she says she can see that her mother is gradually growing weaker and weaker. She is barely able to sit up long enough to have her bed made."

"And how does that noble little Lizzie continue to bear up under her great and responsible duty? I imagined a few days since, when I was in there, that she began to look haggard and thin."

"I haven't noticed it, grandfather. She not only appears to be in good health, but in good spirits, and even cheerful. One who didn't know her would scarcely believe she could appear so cheerful when she is over her sick and dying mother all the time. Her mother says she is just as cheerful when alone with her as when anybody is present, and that she can bear her sufferings much better than if Lizzie was moping and unhappy."

"There are few such girls as Lizzie Swift. She deserves and will receive greater reward for her devotion to her sick mother than this world can bestow."

"She's the best girl I ever saw, grandfather. Only to think of her doing all the work, having all the care of that little wild sister of hers, and nursing her sick mother day and night as she does!"

"It is truly wonderful, and only shows what a young girl, even, can do, if she understands her duty, and her heart is in the work," replied the old gentleman.

"And then she is so thankful for what any one does for her that there is much more satisfaction in helping her than some others. To-day she spoke in particular about the kindness of Tom Sprightly. She says he comes there every day, and some days two or three times. He will talk with her, and try to find out some little thing that her mother thinks she would like, and then off he goes and gets it. Sometimes he will bring her a nice little mess of trouts, and then again a young pigeon. She had no idea that Tom could be so thoughtful, or that he had so kind a heart, till since her mother has been so sick. She said she was not at all surprised at George's kindness, because he is always so thoughtful about everything. What a pity it is, grandfather, that Tom is so wild!"

"O, Tom is a boy of good principles, only he's a dear lover of fun. I've no doubt but that he'll make a good, smart, steady man."

"I hope so," said Lucy, with a good deal of earnestness.

Mrs. Swift was a widow, her husband having been dead about a year. She was left in poor circumstances, with two young daughters, Lizzy and Mary; the former being thirteen at the time of her father's death, and the latter four years younger. Mrs. Swift had been in a slow, lingering consumption for years; and two years before her husband died she had been obliged to refrain from all work, and wholly give up the management of household affairs. Mr. Swift knew not what to do. His circumstances would not allow of his paying a housekeeper and nurse, and the family had no female relative who could devote her services to them.

At this trying juncture Lizzie Swift, then eleven years of age, proved herself a priceless jewel. She had always been of great assistance to her feeble mother, performing all the work she possibly could when out of school. One day, when Lizzie came from school at noon, she found her mother much more poorly than usual, but still attempting to get dinner. The child at that moment made a firm resolve, from which she never wavered. She persuaded her mother to go and lie down, and completed the preparations for dinner herself. When the meal was over, she cleared everything up nicely, and telling her little sister to be sure and stay with her mother till she came back, put on her hat and shawl, and ran away in the direction of the school-house.

In the course of twenty minutes Lizzie entered her mother's room with all her school-books in her arms.

" Why, Lizzie, what have you brought all your books home for?" exclaimed Mrs. Swift.

" O, I have graduated, dear mother," replied the child, with one of her sweet smiles.

" That can't be, my daughter; what do you mean?"

" Well, mother dear, I'm not going to school any more, and you're not going to do any more work. I can and shall do everything myself, with some instructions from you — and I don't mean to trouble you much even for them. Now, don't make one word of objection, dearest," protested Lizzie, with a kiss, seeing that her mother shook her head, " for I've formed a solemn resolution to do everything about house, except washing the clothes, and to do it as well as I can, and to take good care of you, too, kindest of mothers. I am well and willing, and shall try to be your nice little housekeeper and nurse."

Mrs. Swift clasped her precious young daughter in her feeble arms, and burst into tears; but they were the tears of thankfulness.

" Heaven be praised," she fervently uttered, " for

such a daughter — such a ' nice little housekeeper and nurse ' ! "

How well the young girl sustained her position of housekeeper and nurse, — her father having sickened and died during the time, — the reader can in some degree judge from the preceding conversation between Colonel White and Lucy.

The circumstance which first brought the Swift family under the special notice of Colonel White was somewhat peculiar. Shortly after George Herrick entered into his arrangement with the old gentleman, Mr. Swift was employed one day to repair the cellar floor under the colonel's house, and George assisted him. The job was not completed the first day, and Mr. Swift was to come on the morrow to finish it. When they left off work at dusk of the first day, George was particular to shut and fasten upon the inside the outside trap-door that closed the cellar steps leading up into the back yard. As they were passing up the stairs leading to the kitchen, Mr. Swift re-marked that he had forgotten his saw, which he wanted to use at home in the evening, and went back into the cellar for it, George remaining on the cellar stairs. They then passed out together, and Mr. Swift went home.

About half past twelve o'clock that night George

Herrick awoke suddenly, though he did not know from what cause; but he had an impression that he had heard some unusual sound. Listening attentively, he thought he heard footsteps at the back of the house. Jumping from his bed, he moved the curtain slightly at one side of the window and looked out. The distance from his window to the back part of Colonel White's house was perhaps fifty feet, and the ground was shaded by two large old apple trees. At first he saw nothing unusual; but presently a man stepped carefully from behind the tree nearest the colonel's house, and walked stealthily towards the outside entrance to the cellar. When he reached that point he stood for a moment as if listening, and then stooped and took hold of the trap-door. George concluded at once that he was a burglar, and said to himself, —

"Mr. Rogue, you'll be disappointed there, for I fastened that door on the inside myself the last thing before leaving the cellar." Judge of his surprise, then, when he saw the man raise the trap-door and lean it back against its support. George had already commenced slipping on some of his clothes, and a moment after, as the man descended the steps, he cautiously opened the back door, ran lightly across the space of ground, carefully closed the trap-door, and hooked it on the outside, saying to himself, "My fine fellow, I guess you're in a trap."

George then passed carefully round the corner of the house to a private door, of which he had a key given him by the colonel, as he was a very early riser, and often wanted the key to the barn, wood-house, or tool-house before the folks were up in the morning. He went with caution to the old gentleman's sleeping-room, partially opened the door, and spoke his name in a low tone, knowing that he was easy to wake.

"Is that you, George?" asked the colonel, rising on his elbow.

"Yes, sir; hush! there's some one in your cellar. He entered at the outside cellar door, and I have shut and fastened it after him. He can't get out. Let us hurry down cellar, and see what he's doing."

Colonel White got out of bed very carefully, lighted a lamp, slipped on his pantaloons, dressing-gown, and slippers, and took down his scabbard, which hung over the head of his bed, and drew his trusty old sword. Mrs. White slept very soundly, and knew nothing of what was going on. George took the lamp, and the two proceeded silently to the cellar. There were three divisions in the cellar. When they reached the foot of the stairs, they looked all around; but everything was right. George then carefully opened the door leading to the middle cellar, and there stood a man at the pork barrel, holding a small lantern, with a large-sized market-basket at his side, containing a peck or more of potatoes, and into which he was just placing a large strip of salt pork. George whispered to Colonel White, —

" *It's Mr. Swift.*"

" Is it possible?" and the old gentleman seemed for the instant to be utterly confounded.

After a moment or two, however, he made up his mind as to the course he should pursue, and walked straight towards the intruder, who now, for the first time, saw that he was detected; but he made no attempt at escape or resistance. He stood in silence, with downcast eyes.

" Neighbor Swift," began the colonel, " why didn't you tell me last evening that you needed these articles? You could have taken them home with you then, and saved yourself the trouble of coming after them at this hour."

There was nothing in Colonel White's tone that sounded like reprimand or sarcasm. His words were those of genuine kindness; but Mr. Swift still remained silent, and the colonel continued : —

" I am satisfied, neighbor, that there was pressing need in your family, or you would not have come in

this way for these articles. *I* am partly at fault
myself. I knew you to be a poor man, and I should
have paid you last evening for your day's work, or at
least have asked you if you wanted it; but I did not
once think that your family might need it *then*. I
hope you will forgive me;" and the kind-hearted old
gentleman, who *lived* Christianity, extended his hand
to the downcast man whom he had caught in the act
of appropriating his property.

Mr. Swift seized the extended hand, and burst into
tears.

"Colonel White," almost groaned the conscience-
stricken man, "why didn't you run me through with
your sword, as I deserve, instead of treating me thus
kindly? It's true my family are suffering, and I have
been too proud to let the fact be known. I was too
proud last evening to ask you for my pay, but not too
proud to come here *to steal*. Can you understand such
sinful weakness in human nature, Colonel White?"

"Yes, I can understand it, and forgive it," was the
generous reply.

"Colonel White, if you forgive me, I'll ask my
Maker's forgiveness also. This is my first offence of
the kind, and it will be my last. Your generosity, my
kind friend, has saved me."

Mr. Swift then went on to state that he had had

work only part of the time for some weeks; that his wife was sick, and there was but little in the house for his children to eat. He was thinking, during the day, while at work in the cellar, where he saw the large stores of provisions of various kinds, how hard it was that his family should be in need, while others had such abundance. And when evening came, and nothing was said to him about pay, in a moment of despair he said to himself, " I will help myself here to-night ; " and when he went back into the cellar for his saw, he had unfastened the trap-door.

" Well," said Colonel White, " let this be a lesson to both of us. Remember that it is no disgrace to ask assistance of your fellow-man, if you have not brought your distress upon yourself by some wrong-doing ; and never hesitate a moment to ask for your just due when you need it. And I shall never let another poor man that I owe go home at night without offering to pay him. I feel that I was very negligent of my duty. Now, neighbor Swift, take your basket of potatoes and pork," said the colonel, as he stepped into the back cellar and took down a nice chicken from a hook ; " and here is something for your sick wife. Come to-morrow, and finish your job, and receive your pay. This affair will never be known outside these cellar walls unless you make it known yourself."

"O, Colonel White," said the poor man, as he took up his basket, "how can I show my gratitude for this undeserved kindness?"

"By avoiding anything of the like nature again," replied the old gentleman, blandly.

"Who but Colonel White would have treated the man in this kind way?" thought George Herrick, as he went round and opened the trap-door.

Mr. Swift departed, and the colonel and George returned to their beds, nobody but themselves being the wiser for their midnight adventure.

The next morning Mr. Swift came and finished up his work in the cellar, and the colonel kept him employed the remainder of the day upon something else. At night he paid him, and sent George with the horse and wagon to take him home, with a goodly supply of provisions, and some delicacies for his sick wife which Mrs. White had prepared through the day.

From that day forward Colonel White's family never lost sight of the Swifts. On his death-bed Mr. Swift alluded to the above affair, in conversation with the colonel, and said that the kind treatment he then received had saved him from despair and disgrace, and enabled him to work with some heart until his recent sickness. He had subdued his false pride; he had written, a few days before he was taken down sick, to his wife's brother in Chicago, who was a man of property, and by return mail had received a letter containing one hundred dollars, with a promise to render further assistance to the family. His conscience was at case; he trusted in the promises of the gospel, and hoped for happiness beyond the grave. And for all this he felt that he was indebted to the generous treatment and Christian advice he received at that singular midnight meeting in the cellar.

CHAPTER XIII.

THE ADVANCEMENT OF THE "INVINCIBLES."

S the summer of 1861 was passing, with its startling events of victories and defeats in various parts of the country, the boys of Harryseekit were making rapid improvement in military knowledge under the friendly and judicious instruction of Colonel White. The exciting news from the seat of war, from week to week, together with the regular and well-timed suggestions and admonitions of their faithful old instructor with regard to the importance of patriotism at home, served not only to inspire this company of boys to aim at proficiency in their military drill, but also had a most salutary effect in firmly establishing in their youthful minds such a deep love of country and veneration for the Union as would prove an invulnerable shield against the corruptive blight of demagoguism and the more open and sweeping assaults of treason by which they might be assailed in the future.

Colonel White proceeded systematically with his young company. After perfecting them in the proper "position," according to the rules laid down at their first meeting, he instructed them in the motions of the head by the commands, "Eyes right;" "Front;" "Eyes left;" "Front;" "Rest;" "Attention;" and so on. Then came the different "facings," followed by forward marching, and marching obliquely.

In all these lessons the old soldier insisted on precision, and no one of the pupils ever demurred; for all felt an increasing interest in the movement. When instructing them in the different "steps," he would often post himself ten or twelve paces in their front, facing them, and if he could see the sole of a single shoe as the foot was raised or planted, or discover any waving of the upper part of the body, he would tell the pupil that it would not do, and kindly explain the cause and effect of the inaccuracy.

As the colonel kept George constantly in advance of the rest of the company in tactical information, he received much assistance from that intelligent youth in drilling the Invincibles. The result was, that by the combined efforts of the two, the young soldiers were so far advanced in the course of a few weeks, that their instructor imparted to them the gratifying information, at the close of one of their drills, that

9

they might now make application to their parents for a plain blue uniform, arms, and equipments, and report progress on their next drill-day. And he particularly impressed upon their minds his desire that no one would absent himself on account of being unsuccessful.

This information was received with rounds of applause by the happy boys, nearly all of whom had received encouragement from their parents that their hopes would be realized with regard to a soldier's outfit. Many of the good people of Harryseekit, who had thought lightly of the project at first, were now willing to accede to the wishes of their boys, seeing that they took so deep an interest in the movement, and being convinced that it was having a good influence in more ways than one.

Squire Belmont had no children; but both he and his wife had hearts, and they took pleasure in doing their full share towards making the children of others happy. This whole-souled man had talked the matter over with Colonel White, with regard to the boys' outfit, and requested to be informed of every instance where parents were unable or unwilling to furnish the same, pledging himself to raise among his friends, or make up from his own purse, a sum sufficient to accomplish the object. So the colonel knew upon what he was relying when he hinted to the boys that they need not be discouraged if they were unsuccessful in their appeals at home.

The next drill-day arrived, and forty-two of the members of the Invincibles reported that their parents were ready to furnish all that was required. This left only eight to be provided for. Their instructor congratulated the company upon its great success, and informed the disappointed few that Squire Belmont had pledged himself to see that they had their uniforms and equipments with the others. Such cheers as went forth from fifty young throats when this announcement was made, would have done that kind and indulgent gentleman's heart good to hear.

Mr. Cutter, the village tailor, was at once furnished with a good job in making up the uniforms, and, having a taste for patriotism, as well as for "cabbage," he readily agreed to make a deduction of one dollar on each suit from his first price, and warranted that the uniforms should not be made of "shoddy." Every seamstress in town was employed on the uniforms, and many ladies volunteered their services to assist, in order to finish the whole in the shortest possible space of time.

A large number of the boys, and some of their parents, proposed that they should have short, light fire-arms; but that matter was finally left with Colonel White to settle, who decided that they had better order the regular army musket, as the young soldiers would be constantly growing stronger, and their guns would seem lighter and lighter, from week to week, as they continued to practise with them. This, the colonel argued, would be of great importance to them should they be called upon to take the field at some future day.

At the second regular meeting after the above mat-. ter was decided upon, the Young Invincibles appeared in their neat uniforms, with fifty muskets, and all necessary equipments for home drill. And now they began to feel that they were soldiers indeed. In fact, as they stood in perfect line, on that first occasion, with their muskets at shoulder, they did make quite a soldierly appearance. And in justice to their tailor it should be said (we really hope he did not afterwards become an army contractor) that they certainly looked as if they might pass through a north-east storm, and have something besides their knapsacks left on their backs.

Colonel White, in his younger days, had been considered one of the most finished swordsmen in the country; and he had recently taken much pains with George Herrick in the art of fencing, whose eagle eye and steady nerves had made him a most apt scholar; and his teacher soon pronounced 'him a complete master of the weapon.

The boys took additional interest when they began to drill with their muskets, and gave the closest attention to all instructions. Consequently they made rapid progress, and at the end of a few more weeks they understood quite perfectly the ordinary manual exercise; loading and firing without cartridges; loading in nine times, in four times, and loading at will; direct firing, and oblique firing to the right and left; position of the ranks in direct and oblique firing; firing by file; marching, and wheeling to the right and left, and so on.

Colonel White was thus far very much gratified with the advancement of his pupils; and the company began to attract a good many spectators at their drills. He now advised them to elect permanent officers, under whose orders the company should be, subject to his advice at all times, as he would still remain their instructor, and should take pleasure in continuing to give them all the information that was practicable. The colonel declined to make any suggestions as to the most suitable candidates. He believed the boys had sufficient intelligence and discrimination to make a judicious selection for themselves; and they would feel their own responsibility more by acting thus independently. They at once made choice of the following officers : —

Captain, George Herrick ; *Lieutenants*, Charles Sprague, James L. Sherman ; *Sergeants*, Thomas Sprightly, John Wilson, Aaron H. Merrill ; *Corporals*, William C. Hunter, Walter Lovejoy, David C. Crocket, Robert Lincoln.

Horace Copeland and Rufus Prince, two boys who signified their wish to join after the original fifty had formed the company, commenced taking lessons in drumming and fifing, and were, ere long, prepared to act as musicians.

When the list of officers was shown to Colonel White, he appeared to be well pleased, and said he thought a better selection could not have been made ; and he had no doubt but that the company would now improve more rapidly than ever before, as the officers would be likely to feel more pride in its advancement. The colonel's opinion proved to be correct.

It was past the middle of August, and, with other exciting news that was almost daily reaching the North from some of the scenes of conflict, came that of the hard-fought battle of Wilson's Creek, where the rebels were defeated, but with the loss to the Union cause of the young and brave General Lyon.

When drill was over, on the first Wednesday afternoon after the reception of this news, the colonel alluded to the battle, informed the boys that he had known the young and brave General Lyon well before his promotion, and before the war broke out; spoke of his excellence both as a man and an officer, and of the great loss the country had sustained in his death. He then took occasion to remark that certain and rapid promotion awaited scores of patriotic and deserving young men, who should perform their duty faithfully in this war, whether as officers or privates.

The old gentleman's remarks made a visible impression on the young company, for he was one of the few who always know the right words and the right time on all occasions. It was a pleasant afternoon, and quite a number of the neighbors were present, who had been witnessing the drill, among whom were some half dozen ladies, and as many young girls — companions of Lucy White.

As the colonel finished speaking, Lucy came tripping along to him, and placed in his hand a copy of the " Harryseekit Express," published that day, containing an account of the affecting incident — connected with the battle of Wilson's Creek — of the little drummer boy from Tennessee, belonging to a Western regiment, who was discovered on the morning after the

battle, by the sound of his drum, which he was beating
to call attention to himself, having had both feet carried away by a cannon ball; and when found, a dead
rebel soldier, who had been fatally wounded in the
battle, was lying near him, who had kindly, in his last
moments, corded the boy's legs with his own suspenders,
in the endeavor to prevent him from bleeding to death.

In a few remarks introducing this incident, the
editor further alluded to some original lines on the
same subject, in the " poet's corner," signed " T. S.,"
which he said were kindly furnished by a *sprightly*
young member of the Invincibles. The colouel detected the authorship of the lines at once by the
initials and the editor's remark, and calling George —
(we ask his pardon) — *Captain* Herrick, who was an
excellent reader, requested him to read, for the edifica-
tion of all, the affecting little narrative. George readily
complied, and then proceeded to read the versification,
which ran as follows : —

LITTLE EDDIE,

THE DRUMMER BOY OF THE FIRST IOWA REGIMENT.

NEAR Wilson's Creek, at early dawn,
    Where blood had flowed most free,
The guard was startled on his post
    At sound of reveille.

(The horrors of that hard-fought field
  Were fresh on memory's page,
And pondering o'er the bloody lines
  One night had seemed an age.)

When on his ear the sound first broke,
  He thought the *rebel* drum
Was beating up the morning call,
  Just o'er the creek's dark run;
But now, anon, from deep ravine
  Came up both full and clear, —
"Rap-tap, rap-tap, rap-tap, tap, tap!"
  Familiar to his ear.

"Our drummer boy, from Tennessee,
  Is in the vale below!"
The guard quick cried to comrades near,
  "I hear his well-known blow;
We missed him in the thickest fight;
  His name's among the slain;
What joy 'twill cause our regiment
  To welcome him again!"

Then dashing down the steep hillside,
  O'er brush and fallen tree,
The soldier stood, with brimful eye,
  Before dear Eddie Lee.

"Good corporal," the brave boy cries,
  "I hear the brook near by,
But cannot walk a single step,
  Though I am parched and dry."

The stream is reached without delay;
  The cooling water drips,
As back the soldier bears the draught
  For Eddie's fevered lips.
The famished boy clasps quick the prize,
  His raging thirst to slake.
O War! his friend beheld a sight
  To cause one's heart to break!

This youth of twelve, so good, so brave,—
  The pet and pride of all, —
Had lost both feet in carnage dread,
  By ruthless cannon ball!
But not a murmur passed the lips
  Of this poor mangled child,
Whose bleeding form had lain all night
  Exposed in forest wild.

"Good corporal," brave Eddie said,
  "Please have the surgeon come,
To see if he can cure my feet —
  For who will beat the drum?

This man, near by, was very kind;
  These cords he gently tied,
To stop the blood from flowing fast —
  Then sank to earth and died."

He pointed to a plat of grass, —
  " Look! look!" — with feeble breath; —
For there a mangled rebel lay,
  Embraced by icy death.
A man of noble soul was he:
  While life was ebbing low,
To Eddie's side he'd tottered on,
  And checked the crimson flow.

The soldier, fearful of surprise,
  And hearing horses' tramp,
Caught Eddie up in stalwart arms,
  And hastened towards camp.
Too late! a rebel troop draw nigh,
  And cut off all retreat,
" I yield," he cried; " but mercy show
  This brave boy without feet! "

The captain of the rebel troop
  Took Eddie up in front:
" O War!" he cried; " a child like this
  To stand the battle's brunt!"

"My father fell in Tennessee,"
The boy then faintly said;
"He loved the Union; so do I —— "
The drummer boy was dead!

"Tom," said Colonel White, as George finished reading, "I did not believe you capable of such depth of feeling. However much these ‘lines may lack the merit of true poetry, they do credit to your heart."

"I suppose that is the whole trouble with me," replied Tom, in his usual light manner. "All my better feelings lie so *very* deep, that they are strangled before they see the light. Nothing but bubbles reach the surface."

As the Invincibles proceeded to their respective homes that evening, it was with feelings of higher regard for their usually frolicsome young sergeant than they ever before entertained.

CHAPTER XIV.

MASON AND SLIDELL.

AS winter approached, Colonel White suggested to the Invincibles that it would be advisable for them to lay aside their uniforms until spring, except on some particular occasions, as their drill days might often occur in stormy weather, which would subject them to an unnecessary wear and tear, and give them a rusty appearance.

He also offered them the use of a good, dry room over his carriage-house for an armory, which was sufficiently large for their arms and equipments, though there was not sufficient space for drilling; but the colonel proposed to remedy this want by having them use his large barn floor when the weather was too inclement to drill in the open air. By this arrangement the boys would be relieved of the trouble of carrying their muskets back and forth, and could continue to receive instructions without exposure in stormy weather.

Fortunately for the young soldiers, the Wednesday afternoons proved remarkably pleasant through the winter, so that it was not found necessary, in a single instance, to resort to the barn for the purpose of drill. Everything went on finely with them. There was no lack of interest shown either by pupils or teacher. The officers proved to be remarkably efficient, and could now handle the company in a very. creditable manner without assistance; but Colonel White always made it a point to be present, and never failed to find an opportunity to give valuable advice, both in military knowledge and patriotic duty. The boys entertained a high degree of respect and love for their venerable instructor, without a single exception. The great interest he took in them, and his uniform kindness towards them, rendered it almost a matter of impossibility that any different feelings could abide in their breasts.

We are not certain that the Young Invincibles did not enjoy their winter drills even more than they had done those of the preceding summer, for Colonel White often invited them into his house after their exercises were over, where, throwing off all military restraint, without putting on rudeness, they always had a good social time, often made more interesting by the presence of Lucy and some few of her school-girl

companions. Sometimes the colonel would relate interesting reminiscences of the war of 1812; and
occasionally Uncle Bill Ballast would come in and
"spin a yarn" for them, which they always enjoyed
exceedingly, as the old sailor never took offence at the
frequent interruptions he met with from the young and
merry group.

It was early in the month of January, and the boys,
having finished their drill, were assembled in Colonel
White's large, old-fashioned family keeping-room, and
were discussing the case of Mason and Slidell, who
had just been released from Fort Warren, in Boston
Harbor, on the demand of the British government.
Uncle Bill was present, and took strong ground against
giving them up. At the time of their capture by Commander Wilkes, the old sailor was highly delighted, as
he took great pride in all naval achievements; and
the spirited little affair by the commander of the
San Jacinto in taking the two rebel ministers of state
from the Trent, one of the British mail steamers, had
pleased Uncle Bill more than any event of the war up
to that time. And now the fact of surrendering them
to the British authorities was a dash of cold water to
the old seaman's enthusiasm. However, after hearing
Colonel White's arguments on the present occasion in

favor of the measure, he acknowledged that policy demanded it.

"The persistency of the British government in searching our vessels was one of the main causes of the last war with that country, you know, Uncle Bill," said the colonel; "and now, in demanding the surrender of Mason and Slidell, that government virtually abandons the 'right of search,' which it has never wholly given up before; and thus the affair places that country precisely where our government desires it should be placed."

"Yes; I see that we have got them on the windward tack there," replied the old sailor; "but I hate to knuckle a grain to John Bull."

"We should never let pride — not even national pride — stand in the way of right and justice," rejoined Colonel White.

"By the way, Tom Sprightly," said Uncle Bill, turning to that youth, "where is that string of verses you promised to write for me when the news first came about the 'Trent' affair? You said you would give me something to the point, — none of your sentimental stuff, — something that would have a good jolly ring to it, to suit the old sailor boys that I meet when I go down to Capeland."

"I know I did, Uncle Bill," replied Tom; "and

I've been waiting to see how the matter was coming out. I don't think Wilkes should lose any of the honor in capturing them if our government has thought best to give them up — do you, Uncle Bill?"

" Not a bit of it."

" I knew you'd say so, and I've *immortalized* the brave Wilkes for you in these ' railroad lines ' ; " and taking a sheet of paper from his pocket, he rattled off the following at locomotive speed : —

MASON AND SLIDELL.

Two old men of late, —
   Envoys fain would be, —
Stealing from their state,
   Ventured out to sea.

Under British flag,
   Thought themselves secure ;
And full oft did brag, —
   " Union we abjure."

One was bound to France,
   Crying, Cotton *King*,
Round the throne to dance,
   Cutting " pigeon-wing."

10

T'other sought John Bull, —
    On the double-quick, —
Cotton-wool to pull
    O'er the eyes of " Vic."

Wilkes, the brave and bold,
    Heard, by merest chance,
Of these rebels old,
    England-bound, and France —

And, in nick of time,
    Shot across the bow
Johnny Bull's Mail Line;'
    Kicking up a row ; —

Taking the old men,
    Secretaries too,
Left the ship again,
    Bidding " Bull " adieu.

" Johnny's " captain swore,
    Roundly, he would tell
How the Yankee tore
    Mason and Slidell

From the British flag,
    On the great high seas.
Wilkes, the funny wag,
    Answered, " If you please ! "

Now, these rebels bold
   Knew not what to do;
Bound to England Old,
   Soon reached England New.

O, how changed their fate!
   'Stead of royal Court,
Ministers of State
   Shut up in a fort!

Johnny took his stand;
   Sent a note to tell
Lyons to demand
   Mason and Slidell.

Soon came cause to grieve —
   Bull was in the thorns;
Seward, on *qui vive,*
   Seized him by the horns.

" Do you want these chaps? —
   Well, — 'tis very well;
Take them, and their ' traps,' —
   Mason and Slidell."

But said Johnny, " O,
   We don't like this trade;
Thought you would say No;
   Then we'd raise blockade."

Thank you, Johnny, dear;
　Oft there is a slip —
When the draught is near —
　'Twixt the cup and lip.

Do you dread the "birch"?
　Johnny, then repent;
For your "Right of Search"
　Vanished with the Trent.

We've met your demand —
　"Mason and Slidell;"
Take them by the hand,
　Cotton they will sell!

Keep them, if you choose —
　Traitors black at heart! —
Save them from the "noose;"
　Play a two-faced part.

"Bravo!" cried Uncle Bill, as he took the paper
from Tom's hand, and tried to make out some of the
lines without the aid of his spectacles. "Bravo!
Tom; you've hit the nail right square on the head.
It's just what I wanted, for it's got the true ring to it.

' Wilkes, the brave and bold,' "

struck up the old sailor, in an air of his own manu-
facture.

" Now for a story from Uncle Bill," cried Tom Sprightly, "or I'll never write any more verses for him with the 'true ring' to them."

" Yes, yes," chimed in numerous voices, " you must give us a yarn now, Uncle Bill."

" I'll tell you a true story, boys," said the old sailor. " I'm getting to be too old to spin yarns."

" Just think of it!" cried Charlie Sprague — "a *true* story from Uncle Bill!"

" Don't mind him, Uncle Bill," said Tom Sprightly, with apparent indignation. " He's nothing but a stuck-up young lieutenant. We older men know how to appreciate your abilities. Now, *I* believe all your sea stories as firmly as I do Robinson Crusoe."

" O, you're a set of young rogues," replied the old tar, in perfect good nature, " and I should serve you right not to tell you a story at all. But as this *is* true, I guess I'll give you the benefit of it."

CHAPTER XV.

UNCLE BILL'S STORY.

WHEN I first gave up going to sea (commenced Uncle Bill), I lived over to the Point, and used to work about the shipyard, doing odd jobs, and assisting in rigging the vessels after they were launched. The ship-carpenters owned, among them, a good stanch boat, in which they used to make occasional trips (always leaving home at night) down the bay to Capeland, rowing all the distance when the wind was not fair for sailing, where, on the next day, they would buy a boat-load of provisions, and return again at night — thus losing only one day's time, which the difference in the prices of their purchases between the two places made up for, and saved them good many dollars besides.

The distance, you know, boys, is about sixteen miles, and the bay is nowhere more than three miles wide ; so the water was generally very smooth, and when the wind was fair it was quite a fine little sail. As they always took pleasant weather for the trip, and moonlight nights if they could so arrange it, there was no difficulty in keeping their course; in fact, many of the men had been back and forth so often that they thought they could pilot the way on the darkest night that ever was. Occasionally I would take a trip with them, and they always had a good laugh at me because I insisted upon taking my compass; but I told them the laugh would be on the other side some time—and so it proved.

It was in the month of August, and five of the workmen — Johnson, Rogers, Pratt, Stetson, and Smith — decided one Friday to make one of their trips down to Capeland. They usually went in a party of five, divided into regular "watches," one man at the helm, two at the oars when it was necessary to row, and two in "the watch below," as the boat had a good dry "cuddy," where two could sleep comfortably. By this arrangement they all got rest and sleep enough to enable them to go right to work in the yard the same morning they arrived home.

I was at the little wharf when the above-named party was getting ready to start. It was about nine o'clock in the evening. The day had been quite cool for the time of year, with a fresh easterly breeze; but it was then perfectly calm; and, although it was clear overhead, with the moon well along in her first quarter, I felt certain, by the feeling of the atmosphere, that fog was hanging about the bay. So I said to Johnson, —

"If I'm not much mistaken, you'll meet a thick fog before you get two miles down the bay, and I should advise you to take my compass. It's right here in the sail-loft, and I'll get it for you if you'll have it."

"Thank you, Uncle Bill," replied Johnson; "but when I can't find my way down to Capeland without a compass, I'll stay at home, and pay Cheatem his own prices. Besides, old fellow, *you* couldn't find your way to bed without your compass."

This, of course, brought down a laugh from the whole party at my expense, while Smith said, —

"No, no, Uncle Bill, we won't take your compass; for if the fog you speak of comes along before you get up to the house, you might mistake the *light*, and run into Cheatem's by mistake."

This allusion was to Cheatem's bar-room, kept at that time in the back part of his store. But, thanks to our good friend here, Colonel White, I had given up the practice of taking my "grog" long before that day. So Smith's shot fell short of the mark. They continued to laugh at me, and joke me about my compass, however, till they were ready to start, when Rogers called out to me, —

" Now, Uncle Bill, I advise you to lay your course carefully by the compass before you start for home; for we should feel very sorry to hear, when we get back, that you got lost in the fog to-night — whether the fog is from the Bay of Fundy, or from Cheatem's Bar."

" Well, Smith," I replied, " you can joke me as much as you please about my opinion; but I tell you, no seaman would think of going from here to Capeland without taking a compass in his boat. Perhaps you'll learn something by experience before you die."

" Good by, Uncle Bill," said they all, pleasantly, as they pushed their boat off from the wharf; and Stetson added, " I hope it won't be so foggy that you can't find your way to bed."

" Good night. *I* hope it won't be so foggy that *you* can't find your way to Capeland," I replied, as I turned and walked up the wharf towards home, more and more convinced, as I proceeded, that there would be a heavy fog in the bay with the flood tide. I reached home in a few minutes, and " turned in," to dream that Johnson and his companions got lost in the fog, and that I had to take another boat, and my compass, and go and find them.

There was not a breath of wind, and of course the

party in the boat was obliged to use the oars. The "watches" for the night were soon arranged, which gave Stetson and Pratt the first watch below; and they at once turned in, leaving Johnson to stand the first "trick" at the helm, with the other two men at the oars. Having an abundance of time to reach Capeland by daybreak, they proceeded very leisurely down the bay, keeping over towards the opposite and western shore. They had not gone far, however, when Johnson remarked, —

"Uncle Bill was right about the fog, after all. Just see how it is drifting in round Goose Rock!"

His companions rested on their oars a moment, and looked in the direction named.

"Uncle Bill is no fool about the weather," said Rogers, as the two pulled away at their oars again; "but his idea of sticking a compass under everybody's nose is perfect nonsense. Say, Johnson, think you can keep her headed towards Capeland if it is a little foggy?"

"I'd like to see the fog so thick for once that I couldn't find my way up and down Harryseekit Bay," replied the helmsman, with a contemptuous laugh.

"Uncle Bill is troubled somewhat with compass 'on the brain,' I reckon," said Smith, as he pulled away at his oar.

In the course of ten minutes more they were completely enveloped in the fog, losing sight of all the little islands as well as the main shore; but Johnson had no misgivings about keeping the boat headed down the bay, and his companions tugged away at their oars until two hours had expired, when Pratt and Stetson were called, and took their turn at rowing, while Rogers and Smith occupied their places in the cuddy.

"Well, Johnson, Uncle Bill's fog has really come upon us," said Pratt, as he and Stetson pulled away lustily at their oars.

"Yes, Pratt, the old sailor hit it right about the fog," replied Johnson; "but I don't need his compass yet."

"I'm glad you know which way we are going," remarked Stetson, "for I own up that I'm completely in the dark. But if I had been awake all the time, perhaps it would be all right with me."

The next two hours passed away, and the party in the boat saw nothing but water and fog. By this time they should have been near Capeland; but they had seen no object since they lost sight of the little islands by which they could judge of their whereabouts, and even Johnson was now obliged to own up that he didn't know anything about where they were, but thought they must be within two or three miles of their destined port.

It was now decided to have a general consultation; and so Rogers and Smith were called. After talking the matter over for some time, they came to the conclusion that it was useless to attempt to reach Capeland until they could get some landmark; and Johnson proposed that Smith should take the helm, as he was the smallest man of the party, and that the other four should row together smartly for an hour, which would probably bring them to the land somewhere, and they could find out where they were, and take a new start.

The plan was adopted, and the four powerful men tugged away at their oars for more than an hour; but still they made no land; fog and water were all that they could see. They were confident that they had not rowed out to sea between the islands, for in that case there would have been a heavy swell, which they would have noticed at once; but instead, the water continued perfectly smooth. It was now past two o'clock in the morning; and as the men were well tired out by their last hour's hard rowing, and had apparently gained nothing by it, they decided to lay on their oars till daylight.

When day broke, they were much gratified to discover land near at hand, though the fog was still so thick that they could see nothing distinctly. Seizing their oars, however, a few hearty strokes brought them quickly to the beach, where they pulled up their boat and made her fast — glad of an opportunity to stretch their limbs on the shore after their wearisome night in the boat. As daylight increased a little, Smith exclaimed, —

"Look! there's a shipyard, with a vessel on the stocks. I guess we're not a great ways from Capeland, any how, for I don't know of any shipyard till we get pretty well down the bay."

"That's a fact," replied Johnson. "Come, boys, let's find out where we are;" and all five started off to obtain the desired information.

They entered the shipyard at one side just as the earliest workman was entering at the other; and as their eyes rested upon him, they all suddenly stopped, and looked at each other as if greatly surprised. Johnson first found his tongue, and exclaimed, —

"How much that man looks like Sam Lunt! If we hadn't left him at home last night, I could take my oath that that man was Sam."

"He does look a good deal like him," said Rogers; "but I think he is a little taller."

"*I* don't think he's any taller," remarked Stetson; "and see, he's a little lame, just like Lunt."

"He does look something like Sam, I think," said Pratt; "but he's altogether too broad about the shoulders."

"And don't you see that he's lame in the wrong leg?" added Smith, as the man walked along towards the vessel.

"No, I don't," replied Johnson. "The fact is, Smith, you're so completely turned round, that you don't know the right side from the left."

"Well," retorted Smith, "my *brain* isn't so turned as to mistake that man for Sam Lunt, especially when we all know that we left him at Colonel White's ship-yard last night."

"Of course I didn't think it *was* Sam," responded Johnson; "I only said it looked very much like him; and I say so still. However, let's hail the chap, and find out where we are."

They all walked along towards the workman, who now noticed them for the first time, and who, on his part, seemed to show some surprise at this unexpected visit of the boat's crew.

"I say, friend," inquired Johnson, "can you tell us how far we are from Capeland?"

"Well," replied the carpenter, partially turning his back upon the party as he spoke, "I don't know 'zactly how far it is."

"O, we're not particular as to the exact distance," replied Johnson; "tell us *about* how far it is."

"Well, it's a number of miles by land, and a good deal furder by water," responded the workman, as he took off his coat and threw it upon a stick of timber, preparatory to commencing work.

"Confound the fellow, how stupid he is!" said Smith, aside to his companions. Then, in a louder tone, he continued, "Well, friend, what place is this? We got lost in the fog last night in the bay, and don't know where we are."

"What place is it? why, don't you see? —*it's a ship-yard;*" and the man took up his broadaxe, and appeared to be examining its edge very carefully.

"The fellow is a fool, I really believe," said Rogers, in a low voice; "but let's pump something out of him at all events. See what you can do with him, Stetson."

As they gathered up nearer to the man, they did not notice that half a dozen more of the workmen had come into the yard, and were standing in a group just behind them, listening to the conversation.

"My good fellow," commenced Stetson, in a suppli-cating tone, "can't you tell us something near how far it is from here to Capeland?"

"Why, yes," he replied, seeming, all of a sudden,

to have become more intelligent; "it's just about six-teen miles."

"*Sixteen miles!*" repeated Stetson, in amazement. "Are you sure it's so far as that?"

"Yes, I am certain of it," replied the man with the axe.

"That's a good joke," said Stetson, turning to his companions. "We must never let Uncle Bill hear of this. *We have rowed right past Capeland sixteen miles.*"

"It won't be much of a joke, though, rowing back against this strong easterly breeze that's springing up," remarked Pratt.

"You see, my friend," said Stetson, again address-ing the carpenter, — who had grown extremely red in the face, was shaking all over, and looked as if he was going into a fit, — "we started from Harryseckit last evening to row down to Capeland, and, after row-ing all night, this is the first land we made, for we were completely lost in the fog. What town is this?"

The carpenter now turned his face fully upon his visitors, and they all started as if they had seen a ghost. It was Sam Lunt, and no mistake.

"In the name of wonder," exclaimed Johnson, "how came you here, Sam Lunt?"

"In the name of wonder," replied Lunt, "where would you expect to find me?"

"Why, where we left you last night, of course," responded Johnson — "at Colonel White's shipyard."

"Well, I rather guess your *brain* is still in the fog, for *this* is Colonel White's shipyard, *where you have worked for the last ten years!*" shouted Sam Lunt, bursting into a fit of uncontrollable laughter, in which he was joined by the whole gang of workmen belonging to the yard, who had assembled just in time to witness the winding up of the joke.

The light now flashed upon the bewildered party. *They had rowed in a circle all night, and landed just where they started from.* They gave a scream that could have been heard for a mile, and started for their boat. They didn't show their heads in the shipyard again till the next Monday morning. They didn't hear the last about getting lost in the fog in a hurry, I can tell you. But they were all good-natured fellows, and never took offence at being joked about it. And they never laughed at me about my compass again, and never went to Capeland without it after that day.

"And now, boys," continued Uncle Bill, "my true story is ended, and the moral of the whole thing is,

11

Never go to sea without a compass — and let that compass be the 'Good Book'!"

The company had been highly entertained by the old sailor's story, and laughed most heartily at the funny *denouement*. Had they been out doors, they would undoubtedly have cheered Uncle Bill lustily. As it was, they contented themselves by passing him a vote of thanks, at which he appeared to be perfectly well satisfied.

CHAPTER XVI.

THE FRESHET.

NUSUAL quantities of snow had fallen during the winter, most of which had continued on the ground up to the present time, the early part of March. For a few days past, however, the weather had been mild, with indications of rain. It was Wednesday afternoon, drill-day with the Harry-seekit "Invincibles," and, notwithstanding the threatening aspect of the weather and the "slosh" under foot, the members began to assemble as the hour of two drew near, on their usual parade-ground in front of Colonel White's.

It was already beginning to rain, and the colonel considered the state of the weather and the state of the parade-ground sufficient arguments for giving his young soldiers temporary shelter. Accordingly he proposed to them that they should take possession of his large barn floor, which was clear and clean, and of ample dimensions for the required purpose. This proposition was readily assented to by the boys, who did not consider it at all unsoldierlike to retreat before a north-easter that was being heavily reënforced by the old Storm-king himself. Tom Sprightly was the only one who made any objection, declaring, contemptuously, that soldiers who were afraid of getting their skins wet *might* skulk into a barn like a parcel of calves; but they would deserve to be thoroughly cowhided, and to have their names changed to the *Barn-stable Invisibles.* Still, Tom was the very first one to reach cover, turning somersets the whole length of the barn, and making a grand racket generally, in order, he said, to ascertain if Colonel White kept *sound sleepers* underneath the floor.

It was now near the time of roll-call. The boys had not mustered so strongly as usual, on account of the bad walking — many of them living at a distance; and George Herrick had not yet made his appearance. On inquiry being made for him, it was ascertained that he had gone with the horse and sleigh to take Lucy and some of the neighbors' girls up to Squire Belmont's, where the School-girls' Soldiers' Aid Society met that afternoon.

Presently George drove into the yard. The wind had greatly increased, and the rain was now falling rapidly. As he entered the barn, he said to Colonel White, who had that moment joined the boys, —

"I shouldn't wonder much if we should have a freshet, for when I came back over the bridge, I noticed that the water was beginning to rise."

"I don't think the thaw has continued long enough, as yet, to cause any great rise in the streams," replied the colonel. "At all events, not enough to trouble our bridge, which has never been considered in any danger since it was built. The stone abutments are very firm, and the whole structure is stronger every way than the old one that was carried away by the great freshet of 1840."

"Peppermint and shoestrings!" exclaimed Tom Sprightly, pointing out of the barn door; "just see Uncle Bill! Something is in the wind; for who ever saw the old fellow move so quickly before?"

The eyes of all present followed the direction of Tom's finger, and, sure enough, there was the old sailor coming towards the barn at a shambling gait between a walk and a run, but getting over the ground at an exceedingly fast rate for him. Before he reached the party in the barn, he cried out, —

"Colonel White, we must stand watch by the bridge this afternoon, or it will all go by the board! Young Joe Stover has just gone down the Landing road, with his horse on the clean jump, to tell 'em down there to the Lower Mills to make everything taut and fast, for there is a break in the dam at the foot of Miller's Pond, and at the time he left, the water was pouring through it at the rate of ten knots, and they expected the whole thing would go by the board."

Miller's Pond was about four miles above the bridge.

"Attention! boys!" cried the colonel. "We can have no drill to-day. You needn't take your guns from the armory. We shall get our jackets wet, after all. If the dam up to the pond gives wholly away, the entire Interval will be flooded. The ice will break up, and the current will bring it down with such force as to endanger the bridge. You can render much assistance if you don't become too much excited, and will work with some kind of system. Now I propose to form you into working squads, with separate leaders, all to be under the general direction of some one of experience. How many are present?"

"Thirty," promptly replied the clerk.

"Well, let us see. — Uncle Bill, you select seven of the boys to be under your charge; but don't take George Herrick."

Uncle Bill soon made his selection, which included Tom Sprightly.

" Now, I want seven of the younger boys for my-self," said Colonel White.

They at once stepped forward.

" Now, George, you take charge of seven more, and the remaining eight may choose their own leader."

This was quickly done ; and the whole arrangement, which had occupied but a few minutes, being satisfac-torily completed, the party immediately started off to the bridge to see how matters looked. It was found that the ice had not broken up at or near that point, but had crumbled away a little in spots at either shore, and the water was fast overflowing the whole surface of the ice as far as could be seen. And notwithstand-ing the rain was now beating down furiously, and the wind was fiercely whistling among the stately elms in the Interval, yet, plainly above these sounds could be heard the roar of the coming flood and the cracking and crashing of the ice afar off up the river, which was positive evidence that the break was extensive, even if the dam had not been carried wholly away, and that the entire body of water in Miller's Pond was rushing down towards the ocean with overwhelming power.

Colonel White seemed to comprehend all the proba-bilities and dangers of the case at a glance. He saw that the current at the bridge would not be very swift until the Interval had become wholly flooded; but then it would be almost a torrent, for the structure was thrown across the river from hill to hill, and the banks were high and abrupt at each end of the bridge, and so continued for a few rods up stream. The colonel and his party had been the first to reach the spot; but the news had spread, and now men were fast assembling from all quarters. There were several carpenters among the number, who were making a good deal of talk as to what was best to be done. Colonel White stepped up on the end of a pile of timber and planks that lay half buried in the snow near the end of the bridge, — the remains of lumber that had been used in making repairs the autumn before, — and in a tone of voice that all could hear, said, —

"Neighbors, if we expect to save the bridge, we must have a temporary breakwater, or ice-guard, made at once from this timber. It should be a floating raft, in form of a V, resting against the piers, and pointing up stream. — Uncle Bill," continued the colonel, turning to the old seaman, "will you agree to moor a raft safely in that position?"

"Ay, ay, sir," was the brief, but confident, reply.

The idea was readily caught at by the carpenters, and many busy hands were at once engaged in freeing the lumber from the snow, and taking it up the river a few rods, to a spot where the ground sloped gently to the water's edge, affording a suitable place for building the raft, as well as for launching it. The Young Invincibles took hold with a will. One of the carpenters had his saw with him, and another had a hatchet and some nails; so the work immediately commenced on a small scale, while boys were despatched in different directions for more tools, nails, and whatever seemed most necessary for the emergency. Everything seemed to depend upon finishing the raft before the heavy bodies of ice reached the bridge.

As soon as the raft was decided upon, George Herrick took one of his squad, and ran with all speed back to Colonel White's, tackled up the horse and sleigh, collected all the axes, shovels, picks, crowbars, &c., and piled them in, and then drove along to Uncle Bill's boat-shop, knowing that he had followed them home, where they quickly gathered up a lot of ropes, blocks, and other materials of the kind, of which the old sailor always kept a good supply on hand, and, having placed them in the sleigh, all three jumped in, and were soon back to the bridge.

The moment the sleigh was unloaded, George said to Colonel White, anxiously, —

" I have this instant thought of Lucy and the other

girls up at Squire Belmont's. They ought to be home before the bridge is unsafe."

" Well thought of, my boy," replied the colonel, approvingly. " Drive up there as fast as possible, and bring back every girl that lives on this side of the bridge. I am fearful the flood will be upon us before the raft is completed. I will take charge of your boys while you are absent."

The work upon the raft now went on bravely. The Invincibles all seemed to vie with each other in their endeavors to facilitate operations. Their praise was in everybody's mouth. But Tom Sprightly stood out prominently before them all. He had been out in the bay frequently with Uncle Bill in his boat, and had spent many hours at different times in the old sailor's boat-shop, and recollecting all that had been told him on these occasions, he probably knew more about ropes and rigging than any of his companions. Uncle Bill understood this; and 'as soon as he had taken his materials from the sleigh, he said, —

" Tom, I'm going to promote you. A *lieutenant* ain't nothing. I want you to be my *chief mate* this afternoon."

" Thank you, Uncle Bill; I accept the office, and will do the best I can," replied the lad, touching his cap.

The old sailor had no reason to regret the appointment, for Tom not only saw that all of Uncle Bill's orders were faithfully carried out, but he performed prodigies of labor himself. He seemed to be everywhere present, especially if there was any difficult job to be done ; and his unsurpassed agility enabled him to perform many things where another might have failed. With such an efficient mate, and so active a young crew, the old sailor soon had all his preparations made for mooring the raft as soon as it was completed. He then said to Colonel White, —

" We ought to have some kind of communication with the other shore, in case the bridge *does* go."

" I know it," replied the colonel ; " but how can it be done ? "

" Give me one of the carpenters for a few minutes, and I'll soon do the job, with the help of my boys," responded Uncle Bill.

The carpenter came at once, and soon had two strong posts driven through the snow into the solid earth that covered the stone abutment, about four feet from the commencement of the wooden part of the bridge. These posts were side by side, two feet apart. Across the bridge, on the other abutment, two corresponding posts were set. While this was being done, Uncle Bill and Tom measured the distance, and prepared two strong ropes, of the proper length, and stretched them across to the tops of the opposite posts, and made them as taut as possible, about three feet above the bridge. Then all of Uncle Bill's gang of boys set nimbly to work tying short pieces of smaller line across from rope to rope, like the ratlines to a ship's shrouds, but long enough to allow the double to drop down about two feet below the main ropes. These lines were placed about four feet apart. This was a work of a very few minutes, as there were many sets of fingers to perform it. To complete the job, some pieces of thick boards, about ten feet in length and eight inches in width, were run along flatwise through these looped lines the whole extent of the ropes, the ends of each two pieces lapping each other, and being firmly lashed together at these points, and also lashed to the lines in which they were suspended. It was a very simple affair, and its construction occupied but a few minutes' time; still, if the framework of the bridge should be carried away, a person could pass over the chasm — about forty feet — on these suspended lines with comparative safety. The moment it was completed, Tom Sprightly cried out, —

"Hurrah, boys! Just see our Suspension Bridge! I'm going to be the first passenger over it. What's the toll, Uncle Bill?" and springing up, he seized a rope in each hand, and ran the whole length and back again with perfect ease, thus showing the practical working of the experiment.

The probability is, that no horse ever passed over the mile of ground between the bridge and Squire Belmont's in so short a space of time as did Dancing Jim on this occasion. On reaching the house, George waited for no preliminaries, but at once entered the room where the girls were assembled, and said, —

" Young ladies, don't be alarmed ; but there is danger of a great freshet, and I want all of you who live the other side of the bridge to be in my sleigh in just two minutes. Hurry, but don't be frightened."

The girls needed no further urging. They ran quickly for their things, and were soon jumping into the sleigh.

" Is the bridge in danger?" asked Mrs. Belmont.

" Not yet," replied George ; " and men are at work to guard against accident. But the freshet will be very high."

" I remember well when the old bridge was carried away, and I hope the same fate will not attend this," remarked the lady.

The girls were all in the sleigh, and George was ready to jump in, when he turned, in surprise, to Mrs. Belmont, who was standing in the door, and asked, —

" Where is Lucy White? "

" O, she and Julia Lovell went up to Mrs. Grover's before it began to rain much, to get some work that that lady had been preparing for the girls to do this afternoon; and it has rained so fast ever since that I presume she made them stop. Their folks need not worry at all about them, for I know if it don't stop raining soon, Mrs. Grover will send them down here in her sleigh, and I will keep them all night. So you need not expect to see them till the storm is over."

" Thank you, Mrs. Belmont," replied George; " that will make it all right; for I don't see how I can possibly take the time now to go up after them."

" There's no necessity for it," rejoined the lady. " I will be responsible for their safety."

George sprang into the sleigh, and started his horse at a smart trot on his way back to the bridge.

CHAPTER XVII.

A DANGEROUS PASSAGE.

HEN George Herrick reached the bridge with his freight of young school-girls, he was amazed at the change that had taken place during his absence of about twenty minutes. The scene that now presented itself was one of wild and fearful grandeur. The rain was now falling in a complete torrent, and the wind had increased almost to a hurricane. The Interval, which less than an hour since was marked by two distinct streams, with smooth ice surfaces, was now one entire sheet of agitated water and ice throughout its whole length and breadth, or as far as the eye could penetrate through the driving storm, and the water was still rapidly rising.

Cakes of ice, of various forms and dimensions, were hurled along with fearful velocity, — some by the force of the current itself, and others by the fierce north-east wind, — dashing and crashing against each

other, against the trees, and against the bridge itself,
with fearful force.   Fortunately, no heavy masses of
ice had yet struck the piers, though several had been
forced heavily against the abutments ; but these were
of solid masonry, and there was no danger of their
starting.   The current, which had increased to a
mighty torrent, was pouring through the sluice-way
under the bridge with the roar of distant thunder, and
being full of small cakes of ice, which were inces-
santly dashed, with great force, against the piers,
caused the whole framework of the bridge to tremble,
twist, and reel, as if in imitation of those grand old
elms of the Interval, which had withstood the storms
and floods of centuries, but which were now waving
and writhing in the fierce gale, and plunging their
lowermost branches into the foaming waters at their
base, which had encroached far up their massive
trunks, leaving them standing forth, in all appearance
to the eye, like a forest in an ocean.   It was a scene
for the pencil rather than the pen.

George drove directly upon the bridge, with the
intention of crossing at a quick trot ; but, as the horse
neared the wooden part of the structure, he hesitated,
shook his head, shied, and finally stopped short.   The
girls also began to show symptoms of fear.   The
approach of the horse and sleigh had been noticed by

the working party on the other side, and several of their number, among whom were Colonel White and Tom Sprightly, advanced on the opposite abutment. The colonel called out, —

"George, I don't think there is any danger of the bridge at the present moment; but still, as the horse is shy, and the girls seem to be alarmed, I wouldn't try to cross with such a sleigh-load. Back a little, and let the girls get out, and Tom will show them how to cross."

Tom Sprightly sprang upon the suspension bridge, and taking a rope in each hand as before, ran quickly to the other end of it, greatly to the surprise of the girls, and the approbation of George Herrick, who had not before noticed the suspended structure.

"Capital! Whose idea is that?" asked George.

"Uncle Bill's, of course," replied Tom. "Just give the old fellow *rope enough*, and he'd rig a plan to get up to the moon. Come, girls, hurry up here!" And he lifted one of them into the end of the swinging bridge. "There," he continued, "take a rope in each hand, same as I did, and walk right ahead. There isn't a bit of danger."

As Uncle Bill's suspension bridge was not more than twelve inches above the bridge proper, and as that structure still held together, the girls did not make

12

much hesitation, and in a few minutes all had passed over in safety.

"Where is Lucy?" anxiously inquired Colonel White and Tom Sprightly in the same breath, as the last girl crossed the bridge.

George explained, and both were satisfied, feeling thankful that Lucy had escaped exposure to the drenching storm, which had rendered the situation of the other girls anything but enviable.

George Herrick now jumped into the sleigh again, seized the reins and whip, and said, —

"Come, Dancer, you *must* go over this bridge now — you and I are alone. Go!" and he gave him two smart cuts with the whip.

The horse knew the firmness of his driver too well to hesitate, and he was over the bridge and half way up the hill before George could stop him. But, as he never allowed the horse to have his own way in matters of this kind, he turned him, and drove back to the end of the bridge; turned again, and made the animal stand perfectly quiet, while he helped all the girls into the sleigh again. Then, turning to Colonel White, he said, —

"You are wet through and through, sir. I think you had better drive home and change your clothes, and not come out again — for the present at least."

" Thank you, George," replied the colonel ; " but I can't do it. I must see this matter through."

" Well, then," rejoined the lad, " please ask some one to drive the horse up to the house, for *I* have done nothing at all yet. I must go to work."

Colonel White requested one of the smaller boys to jump into the sleigh and drive up to his house, and say to Mrs. White that she had better keep all the girls there, except those who lived very near, till the storm was over, or he came home. The boy at once complied, and George Herrick cast his eyes about him to see what had been accomplished, and what remained to be done. The raft appeared to be about completed, and was partially afloat, and contained a number of axes, picks, crowbars, and two of Uncle Bill's long-handled boathooks. The carpenters were at work, strengthening it in various ways, yet seemed to be merely improving their time while waiting for some other part of the arrangements.

The raft had been constructed after the plan suggested by Colonel White, the idea being to moor it about midway the current, with some of the most powerful men upon it, close to the piers of the bridge, and as the large masses of ice came down against the point of it, which was armed with a large crowbar, firmly secured so as to allow it to project ten or twelve

inches beyond the woodwork, the men were to chop the
ice-cakes sufficiently small to allow of their passing
through between the piers of the bridge.   Uncle Bill
had all his ropes attached to the raft, leading off in
different directions ; but still it was not pushed out into
the stream.

Some three or four rods up stream from where the
raft lay was a little hillock that overlooked the Interval.
At this point stood Uncle Bill, Tom Sprightly, and two
or three others, all intently looking at some object in
the water, at a considerable distance from the shore.
George Herrick ran up to the old sailor, who stood
with one hand over his eyes, to shelter them from the
driving storm, and said, —

"Uncle Bill, what is the raft waiting for?   It seems
to be about finished."

" It is waiting till we see where that big ' iceberg '
goes, my boy," answered the old seaman, pointing in
the direction of two large elms, that stood near together
directly at the little bend in the river.   " If that should
break loose and come down in a body in the swift current, it would swamp that raft and all hands on it in
a moment, and carry the whole bridge away by the
board."

George looked in the indicated direction, and saw
that the ice was piled up between these two trees

nearly to the height and size of a small two-story house. The current directly above this bend was very rapid, and as the larger cakes of ice came whirling down through it, instead of following the curve of the river, their momentum was such as to cause the larger number of them to shoot straight ahead into the stiller water; and some of the first having wedged fast between these two elms, others, as the water rose, were thrown against and upon them, until the accumulation was sufficient to warrant Uncle Bill in styling it an "iceberg.".

The collection of ice at this point, and the fact that many other large masses had drifted before the wind across the Interval and lodged against, the shore, probably had saved the bridge thus far. But now the huge mass of ice between the two trees was lifting and heaving, and surging violently from the effects of wind and water upon it, and threatening every moment to break away from its tree-bound fastening. Should it do so, the wind would force it again into the current, and the fate of the bridge would in all probability be sealed.

Colonel White and a few others now joined the little party of observation, and the colonel said to Uncle Bill, —

"Do you think of any thing that can be done to

forward matters? The bridge is wrenching and twisting badly. Some of the cakes of ice have wedged in among the piers, holding the water, and thus causing more strain. I think the bridge is in greater danger than at any previous moment."

"I don't know what we can do," replied the old sailor, almost despairingly. "If we only had a boat of any kind, we could put off and cut that iceberg all to pieces. If I had ever expected to see such a respectable little bay of water as this here, I would have had a boat all ready. But who ever thought that these two little pipe-stem brooks could cause so much danger as this? The fact is, colonel, if I was only out there on the water, I should know just what to do; but the land is a mean place to navigate."

"You have done nobly to-day, Uncle Bill," rejoined Colonel White; "so do not underrate your own abilities. All hands give you much credit."

"It's very little that an old sea-dog like me can do on the land," returned the seaman.

"George," said the colonel, turning to that lad, who stood in deep thought, still looking out upon the flooded Interval, "I have often profited by your suggestions. Have you anything to offer now?"

"I have been thinking of something, sir. Uncle Bill," continued he, as he turned towards the dejected-looking old sailor, "you have often told me that when you managed one of the guns ōn board of 'Old Ironsides,' you could plant a shot just where you pleased. Do you think you could hit that pile of ice?"

"Just as certain, my lad," replied the seaman, brightening up a little, "as you could toss an apple on to that raft."

"Then, boys," cried George Herrick, with animation, "we'll bring one of the old field-pieces here from the gun-house, and if that iceberg gets clear of the trees, Uncle Bill shall batter it all to pieces!"

"Good!" ejaculated the old sailor; and he brought his heavy hand down with such force upon the lad's shoulder as to cause him fairly to wince.

"The gun-house! the gun-house!" was now shouted from all quarters; and, as the man who had charge of the building was present, Tom Sprightly ran to him and obtained the key, which he happened to have in his pocket, and at once led the way to the gun-house, followed by nearly all the boys, and a considerable proportion of the men. The building was situated on the main street, some little distance from Colonel White's, towards the Corner. Tom reached the house, and had one of the guns ready to run out the door before anybody else arrived. He examined the limber-box, which contained a dozen or more cartridges of powder, and in one corner of the room he found a considerable number of balls, that were kept for target practice ; and from these he tossed as many as he thought would be needed into the box with the cartridges.

By this time his companions began to arrive, and they ran the gun out and started off towards the bridge. One man had taken the precaution to bring a long rope, which they fastened to the carriage, so that all hands could pull. But the snow was completely saturated with the heavy rain, and the wheels sank deep into it, so that it was both hard and slow work to drag the gun along.

George Herrick had anticipated this very trouble, and, though not so swift in the race as most of his companions, had prepared to obviate the difficulty. As the men and boys were slowly floundering along through the slosh with the gun, up rode George on Old Noll. He was speedily tackled to the carriage, and off they now went at a quick trot, and soon reached the bridge, where they placed the gun in position under Uncle Bill's direction.

"Now, boys," said the old sailor, all animation at the brightening of the prospect, "just as soon as I get this old handcart of a thing loaded, we'll start off the raft, and then if that lubber of an iceberg comes down upon us, I'll blow him out of water. I don't think much of this old stove-pipe, any way," he continued, looking somewhat contemptuously at the gun, " but I'll do the best I can. If I only had one of Old Ironsides' 'barkers' here, I should know just exactly what I *could* do ; " and Uncle Bill went through the process of loading the cannon with the expertness of a practised gunner, taking great care that the powder did not become exposed to the rain.

"Are you going to blaze away at it where it is, Uncle Bill?" asked Tom Sprightly, who was anxious to see what effect a shot would have upon the mass of ice.

" No, no, mate ; as long as the chap hangs there he can't trouble us any ; but if I should cut him loose, he'd come sailing down here, and we should have just so much more ice to look after. If he comes out of his own accord, though, to give us fight, then I'll show him what old Bill can do. I shouldn't be surprised if he was under sail before ten minutes. Tom," continued the old seaman, " you just keep an eye on the lubber, while I see to moving the raft out into the stream."

In less than five minutes Uncle Bill had the raft wholly afloat, the selected crew upon it, and everything in readiness to drop it down into its proper position by the bridge, which was now twisting and reeling under the force of the current and the rapidly accumulating ice. At this moment, when the men had commenced slacking away the lines that held the raft to the shore, they were startled by an outcry from Tom Sprightly, that seemed to be a combination of astonishment, fear, and anguish of mind. Everybody rushed to the spot where Tom stood, near the gun. They were not held in ignorance of the boy's alarm, for their blood grew chill as they looked out upon the water directly to windward, and there beheld a cake of ice, apparently ten or twelve feet square, occupied by two young girls! The larger one of the two might have been about thirteen years of age, while the other was some two or three years younger. The former stood firm and upright, using a large, closed umbrella with one hand as a brace against the ice, to prevent being blown from her slippery foothold, while the other arm encircled her more timid companion, who, from fear or cold, or perhaps both, appeared to be nearly helpless.

Colonel White had a small spy-glass in his pocket, which he at once brought into requisition for the purpose of identifying the girls. He almost instantly lowered the glass, and all color forsook his cheeks as he turned to George Herrick and said, —

" Those two girls are our Lucy, and Julia Lovell."

"I know it," replied George, who was talking earnestly with Tom Sprightly ; " Tom and I knew it from the first. What shall we do ? Tom declares he will swim off to them ; but I tell him he could render them no assistance, even if he lived to reach them, in this ice-cold water."

" No, no, Tom ; that would be of no use. And as the wind blows directly this way, it would be impossible to move the raft in that direction. May Heaven protect them, for we cannot ; " and the old gentleman seemed about to sink to the ground.

The piece of ice on which the two girls were making their perilous voyage was floating along in a moderate current, that set across that part of the Interval from the smaller and more distant stream. This current curved round towards the little prominence from which the anxious friends now gazed, — but yet a few rods from it, — and then joined the main current near the bridge. All seemed to realize that unless Lucy and Julia were rescued before they reached the swift-flowing water, their fate would be sealed. Uncle Bill seized a coil of small rope, and advanced to the brink of the bank, crying out, —

" Keep perfectly still — I want to hail the girls."

" Silence ! all ! " shouted Colonel White.

Uncle Bill's stentorian voice went forth, —

" Lucy White, a-h-o-y ! "

"What is it, Uncle Bill?" came back clear and distinct before the driving storm.

" Sit right down on the ice with your back to the wind, open your umbrella for a sail, and you'll come ashore safe ! " shouted the old sailor.

The instantaneous compliance with the order showed that Lucy understood it; and Uncle Bill was warmly praised by the interested spectators as they saw, in a few moments, that the umbrella-sail was steadily, though slowly, moving the ice-cake out of the current and directly towards them.

While the crowd of friends stood anxiously watching and silently praying for the safety of the two young girls, George Herrick and Tom Sprightly were engaged in a confidential conversation apart from the others.

" George," said the latter, " I fear that this plan of Uncle Bill's won't succeed; and if it don't, I shall not wait another moment, but mean to swim off to the girls and carry a rope."

" It's a noble resolution, Tom, and if you were not here I should attempt it myself, now they are some nearer the shore. But there is great danger from the extreme coldness of the water, the floating ice, and the strong current. If I could swim as you can, Tom, you shouldn't attempt it. But *you* will succeed, if anybody can."

" I shall do my best, any way, George, if I have to undertake it. If I fail, you'll have to say, ' Good by, poor Tom ! ' "

" You *won't* fail, Tom ;" and George clasped his whole-souled young companion by the hand.

" I hope not, George ; but if I do, just tell aunt Huldah and uncle French that they must try to forgive me if I have sometimes carried my jokes too far, for I'm really thankful for all their kindness to me, and shall think of them in my last moments."

" O, Tom, I hope there will be no occasion to deliver your sad message ! " exclaimed George, still pressing his young friend's hand.

" There is one more message ; " and Tom turned his face away to conceal his emotion. " If Lucy White is saved, and I should perish, just tell her that I willingly gave my life in trying to save *her*."

" Tom, Tom," exclaimed George, " I did not know before that Lucy was so *very* dear to you ! She is one of the best of girls, and I love her as I would an only *sister*."

" She *shall* be saved ! " cried Tom, almost frantically.

The two boys now rejoined the old sailor. The floating ice-cake had neared the shore considerably, and Uncle Bill was just making ready to throw the rope, when a most violent gust of wind took the umbrella and fairly lifted Lucy to her feet.

" Catch hold of me, Julia, or I shall blow away ! " she screamed.

The danger aroused her companion, and she clasped Lucy around the waist. The wind proved to be too much for the umbrella, however, for it instantly turned, and the covering was rent in all directions. Uncle Bill threw the line with all his strength, but it fell short of its aim, and he sadly shook his head as he leisurely hauled it in again.

CHAPTER XVIII.

TOM GOES TO THE RESCUE.

"UNCLE BILL," exclaimed Tom, as he drew off his heavy boots, and cast aside his coat, "fasten the end of that rope round me in the right place, for I'm going to take a swim."

"I can't say no, my brave lad, for I should have done the same thing myself at your age," replied the old seaman, as he knotted the line around Tom's slender waist, but in such a manner that it could be easily unfastened when occasion required.

The determined youth instantly sprang down the steep, slippery bank, and plunged into the water. But the whole shore was lined with small pieces of floating ice, extending out thirty or forty feet, which were not large enough to walk upon, and were too near together to permit one to swim among them with any speed or safety. Tom was one of the best of swimmers, but he floundered badly in the ice, without making much headway, and was about to dive and endeavor to swim

out beneath it, when George Herrick, who had anticipated the difficulty, came rushing down to the water's
edge, with his squad of Invincibles, bearing two long
boards, which they instantly ran out from the shore on
the floating ice, thus making a platform for Tom, by
which he quickly reached the open water, and plunged
boldly in, striking out manfully in the direction of the
ice-cake, which was now floating steadily away again
towards the swift current.

The bold swimmer still encountered difficulties. The
water was piercing cold; he was encumbered with
clothing; the weight of the rope was no little drawback; and, in addition, there were frequent pieces of
floating ice, which he had to avoid by making little
circuits; and these pieces of ice would occasionally
strike the line, giving him a sudden pull, and partially stopping his headway. But, as already stated,
Tom was a first-class swimmer, and in warm weather
this would have been mere pastime for him. Under
the present circumstances, however, his energies were
taxed to their utmost; but his heart was in the effort,
and he had determined to do or die. Hence he over-
came all obstacles; and his friends on shore sent up a
joyful shout as they saw the brave youth reach the
object of his destination, and, with Lucy's helping
hand, clamber upon the floating ice.

THE RESCUE. — Page 192.

"O, Tom Sprightly, I thought it was you! but what a risk you have run!" exclaimed Lucy, still holding his hand, as he with difficulty raised himself upon his feet, wet and chilled as he was.

"O, Lucy White, I *knew* it was you! and what risk *wouldn't* I run?" replied Tom, as he gently disengaged his hand and quickly untied the rope from his waist.

Julia Lovell had become wholly discouraged after the accident to the umbrella, and being completely chilled through, she sat upon the ice in a kind of stupor; but Tom aroused her by calling out, —

"Here, Julia, just catch hold of the rope with us, and we'll be ashore in a very few minutes. Come, quick!" and he shook her gently by the shoulder.

The child started, and with considerable effort rose to her feet. All three then took hold of the rope, braced themselves as well as they could, and Tom cried out at the top of his voice to Uncle Bill to "haul in."

"No, no; that won't do — we can't tell how hard to pull, and we might haul you all off the ice," shouted the old sailor in reply. "I have belayed the line, and you must all three pull with might and main."

Tom realized the mistake he had made, and at once complied with Uncle Bill's order; but their ice-cake

13

had now entered the margin of the large, rapid current, and Tom's strength, somewhat reduced by cold and exertion, with the feeble aid rendered by the two small girls, was not sufficient to overcome the force of the water; and the watchful old seaman had to slack away the line continually to enable the occupants of the floating piece of ice to retain the end of it, as they drifted farther and farther away.

Tom well knew, if they once passed into the swiftest part of the current, nothing more could be done; but there was no projection upon any part of their slippery foothold to which the rope could be made fast, and there was nothing at hand that could be driven into the ice as a pin. He thought of the broken umbrella, which he had seen lying on the ice a few moments before; perhaps he could use the handle of that; but it was now gone — having either been blown or pushed accidentally overboard. Whatever was done must be done without a moment's delay. Tom thought of a last resort, and shouted with all his might, —

"Uncle Bill, give me all the slack you can in a moment!"

The line was instantly slacked all away, and Tom rapidly hauled in three or four fathoms of it, stepped to the edge of the ice-cake farthest from the shore, and quickly fastened the end of the rope around his hips.

He then took a position that brought the rope directly across the centre of the cake of ice, and shouted to Uncle Bill to "haul in, lively!" The moment the line began to tighten, Tom dropped himself into the water up to his hips, with his face towards the shore, his arms and upper part of the body extended upon the ice-cake, and the lower portions underneath it — thus forming a sufficient curve to give the line a purchase over the edge of the ice. He then called out again to the old sailor, "Haul in, all the rope will bear," at the same time instructing Lucy and Julia to stand as near the opposite edge of the ice as was safe, and hold the rope down as much as they could, thus keeping it across the centre of the ice, and preventing that from turning, as well as counteracting in a great degree the *lifting* effect upon himself, which might possibly draw him up on the ice, and thus defeat the whole object, as would also be the case if the ice-cake turned. But Uncle Bill had guessed out Tom's ingenious expedient, and the line was taken down on the low ground near the water's edge, thus diminishing the danger of either of the contingencies which the self-sacrificing youth wished to guard against.

Tom's plan worked admirably; and he and his companions began to feel their hopes revive, as they realized that they were moving steadily towards the shore,

propelled by many strong arms under the impulse
of yearning hearts. They had scarcely commenced
moving, however, when Lucy exclaimed, —

"Look, Tom, look!" and pointed up stream.

The lad turned his head in that direction, and saw,
not more than fifty yards distant, the large mass of ice
that had been lodged between the two elms coming
down directly upon them in one entire body. Both
that and the bridge had been forgotten by all during
the last fifteen minutes, in their greater excitement
and anxiety on account of the perilous young voyagers
on the floating ice. But the new danger was now
observed from the shore, and Uncle Bill said hastily
to those who were hauling on the rope, —

"Pull strong, boys, but steady!" and then rushed
to the gun, calling to Colonel White, George Herrick,
and one or two others, who were not easily excited, to
follow him.

"Don't be frightened, girls, they are going to fire a
cannon," said Tom Sprightly, speaking with a good
deal of difficulty, being greatly exhausted from his
almost superhuman exertions, and chilled through and
through by the ice-cold water. The rope might be
severing him in halves for all he knew, as he was so
much benumbed that he had ceased to feel it at all.

"Dear Tom," said Lucy, looking with pity and

admiration at him, *perhaps* unconscious of the endear-
ing term she had made use of, "you will certainly
freeze if you remain there any longer. Can't we pull
ourselves ashore now if you get upon the ice?"

"No, Lucy; we must remain just as we are till we
reach the shore. I can stand it. And if I should
freeze as I am, the rope would hold all the same;"
and the poor fellow smiled somewhat ghastly.

"O, it's too bad!" said Lucy and Julia in the same
breath — the latter having revived a little as the
prospect brightened.

Uncle Bill, with the assistance of his companions,
changed the position of the gun slightly, quickly sighted
it, applied the match, and the ball sped on its swift
errand. As the smoke instantly passed away before
the fierce gale, a loud huzza went up from the party
near the water's edge, as the iceberg rolled heavily
from the well-directed shot, trembled for a single
moment, and then separated in three pieces — the
smaller two rolling wholly out of the current, subsequently floating away before the wind to the shore,
while the main mass continued on towards the
bridge.

"Well done, old land-lubber!" exclaimed the successful gunner, patting the cannon as if it had been
some creature endowed with understanding; "I guess

one more shot will settle that fellow.   We'll learn him
to try to run the blockade ! "

The old sailor instantly proceeded to load the gun
again, growing warm and excited under the renewal
of an occupation long since laid aside.   In the mean
time Tom Sprightly and the two girls were being
drawn steadily, but slowly, towards the shore, for
Lucy had entreated them, when near enough to be
heard, not to pull too hard, as the *rope was fast to
Tom's body.*

" Now, boys," cried Uncle Bill, as he aimed the gun
the second time, " we'll plump that fellow midships,
and see how he'll like that ; " and again the old field-
piece belched forth its flame and smoke, planting the
ball precisely where the gunner's remark had indicated ;
but the ice was firmer than he had supposed it to be,
and although the mass reeled under the shock, and the
chips of ice flew in all directions, still it continued to
float on towards the bridge.

" That will never do," exclaimed Uncle Bill, somewhat disappointed at the effect of the shot; " but I
see his weak point now, and will give him a settler
next time ; "   and he prepared to load for the third
shot.

" You must manage the gun without the help of
George and me this time," said Colonel White, " for

Tom and the girls are close to the shore, and we must attend to them."

The ice-cake with its living freight had nearly reached the shore, and as George Herrick had taken the precaution to have more boards and planks placed there immediately after Tom's departure, they now had a very good floating platform all the way from the open water to the bank.

" O, my dear, dear child! " exclaimed the colonel, as he reached the ice-cake, and clasped Lucy in his arms; " thank Heaven that your life is preserved! At one time I gave you up as lost. But Tom, the noble fellow, has saved you! "

George Herrick had merely pressed Lucy's hand for an instant as he passed her in silence, and was already lifting her preserver upon the ice.

" Tom, can you speak? " inquired George, anxiously, as he endeavored to place the poor fellow on his feet.

" Yes, but I cannot stand," he replied, faintly; and George observed that he remained in the same bent position that he had occupied over the edge of the ice.

" Never mind trying to stand, Tom; I can carry you; " and George Herrick caught him up in his strong arms as if he had been an infant, and bore him towards the shore, followed by Colonel White,

Lucy, and Julia, the latter, also, having to be carried by one of the men, as she was so much chilled that she could scarcely stand.

At this moment the old cannon spoke for the third time, and a shout of triumph mingled with the storm, as a large shelving piece of the iceberg was cut entirely off, thus destroying the equilibrium of the remainder, which rolled wholly over, launching cake after cake of ice from their respective positions, until apparently no two remained connected.

George Herrick, with his usual foresight, had sent one of the boys for the horse and sleigh, which now stood waiting at the end of the bridge. Lucy and Julia were speedily placed in the sleigh, and snugly wrapped up in a buffalo robe. Tom soon followed, brought along by George and one of the carpenters. Then the colonel and George both jumped into the sleigh, and in less than five minutes the girls and their preserver were in Colonel White's house, undergoing a change of garments, and partaking of stimulating beverage. All were soon in a comfortable condition. Even Tom Sprightly began to move about the room, although he could not yet stand up straight.

As soon as George Herrick saw that both his friend Tom and the girls were free from any immediate danger, he hastened back to the bridge, having, by much earnest persuasion, induced Colonel White to remain at home. He found that immediately after Uncle Bill had fired his last gun, he had ordered the raft into position, and that the men, in a very few minutes, had succeeded in clearing away the ice that had lodged against the piers of the bridge, thus greatly lessening the pressure of water upon it, and were, at the time he arrived, manfully battling the large cakes of ice as they came down against their raft — cutting them in pieces, and guiding them through among the piers with their long boathooks.

The rain had now nearly ceased, the wind had lulled considerably, the large masses of floating ice were less frequent, and the rapidity of the current had evidently somewhat abated. Presently Uncle Bill shouted, —

"Hurrah, boys! our work is almost done. The water is beginning to fall, and *the bridge is safe!*"

Three cheers were instantly given by the whole crowd.

It was observable, by looking at the abutments of the bridge, that the water had receded three inches. Miller's Pond, evidently, had been drained; and as the rain had ceased, the water from the melting snow would do no damage. The raft was drawn back to the shore, and, as the sun went down that evening, those wet, tired, and hungry men and boys of Harry-seekit — who, during four long hours, had so bravely struggled against that sweeping flood, subjected all the while to a merciless north-easter — gathered up their implements, and marched in a body up to Colonel White's, leaving the old field-piece that had done such good execution to keep silent guard over the still flooded Interval.

They halted in front of the colonel's house for the purpose of informing him of the fall of the water and the safety of the bridge, as well as to inquire after Tom Sprightly and the two girls whom he had so nobly rescued at the risk of his own life. They were also interested to learn — as the reader may be — how Lucy and Julia came to be placed in their perilous condition on the floating ice. Colonel White had the happiness of informing them that both Tom and the girls were improving fast. He also, in a few words, explained the mystery of the sudden appearance of Lucy and Julia on the floating ice.

On their way from Squire Belmont's to Mrs. Grover's, the girls had been met by young Stover with the news of the expected freshet. He alarmed them by saying that the bridge would probably be carried away before they could get back to it, and that they had better go right down the lane close by, where he had just crossed the rivers on the ice, and cross over as quick as possible, and go up into the road the other side, and go home that way, and he would tell Mrs. Belmont, as he passed the house, that they had gone home. The girls ran down the lane with all haste; but the young man was so anxious to reach the Landing, that he forgot to call at the squire's, and consequently Mrs. Belmont supposed they were remaining at Mrs. Grover's on account of the rain.

The girls crossed the first river without any trouble; but when they reached the farther side of the second, which at this point was only a few rods from the first, they found the ice so much broken up at the shore that they could not get upon the land. They ran first up stream and then down; but the condition of things was the same. They then ran back to the spot where they had entered upon the ice, thinking they would get ashore, at all events. They were much alarmed, however, to find that the ice had also separated from the shore there, and they could not get back. All they could do now was to run down the river, looking on either side for a place where they could reach the shore. But there was no such place to be found. The ice was now heaving and cracking in every direction, and before they were aware of it they had reached the extremity of the ice, and below them was all open

water! They turned to retreat; but at that moment
the ice on which they stood separated from the main
body, and the two little girls found themselves floating
slowly down stream, — where they were finally discovered and rescued as already related.

The colonel finished his explanation concerning the
two girls, thanked the men and boys for the good
service they had performed that afternoon, and the
party was about to leave, when Squire Belmont
drove up to the door. He had been absent all day on
business in the next town, and knew nothing of the
freshet till he reached home. As his wife had heard
nothing from Lucy and Julia, he at once drove up to
Mrs. Grover's, and was considerably alarmed on learning that they had not been there. He then drove down
to the bridge with all haste, and finding that safe, and
no one there, he had continued on to Colonel White's
to gain the desired information.

The colonel relieved Squire Belmont's anxiety about
the girls, and then gave him a very concise account of
the afternoon's work. The squire complimented all
for the faithful manner in which they had performed
their arduous duties, thanked Uncle Bill, in the name
of the county, for his good services, and was particularly complimentary to Tom Sprightly for his noble

deed. Noticing that Tom could not yet straighten up, he said to him, jocosely, —

" My boy, you could hardly turn a somerset now — could you ? "

" I can as soon as I thaw a very little more," replied Tom. " You see, I got one about half turned, and froze — something like the man's keg of powder, that took fire, and burned half up before he could put it out."

" Well, Tom," rejoined the squire, laughing, " I hope you'll *get straightened out* soon, and be able to come up to my house."

" Thank you, Squire Belmont," returned Tom ; " but I'm a little afraid I should meet with another *bull run* affair."

" Tom is getting better fast," said George Herrick, " for his jokes are beginning to thaw out."

The crowd now dispersed, glad enough to reach their warm firesides after their exciting afternoon's work.

CHAPTER XIX.

THE HOUSE OF MOURNING.

IT was near the middle of May, and all nature, as if by magic, had within a few brief days started into active, cheering, blooming life; but in the midst of all this beauty, within the walls of a small house in Harryseekit, an ever-living soul was fast approaching that moment when the last band that bound it to its earthly tenement would be severed, and it would wing its flight to its eternal home in heaven.

Mrs. Swift had continued gradually to sink away, until it was evident to all, herself included, that a few days, at the farthest, must terminate her sufferings. One day, when George Herrick had made his accustomed call, he thought he observed a marked change in the sick woman, and said to the daughter, —

"Lizzie, how would you like to have my mother come and stop with you a few days?"

"O, I should be forever thankful for it," replied the

young girl, as her eyes filled with tears. "I have had numerous offers from the kind neighbors, within a few weeks, to come and stay with me; but I have not thought it necessary to trouble them. Now, I suppose I ought not to be alone, and I should prefer your mother to any one else."

"I know she will come at once, although I have said nothing to her about it," was George's reply.

In less than an hour Mrs. Herrick was assisting the devoted Lizzie in her angelic ministrations at the bedside of the dying woman. The physician informed Mrs. Herrick that the patient could not live the day out. George had so decided in his own mind before he went for his mother, and when she now stated to him the doctor's opinion, and told him she would like to have him remain with her during the day, unless Colonel White had something of much importance for him to attend to, he replied that he had already decided to do so, if Lizzie wished it, and had informed the colonel to that effect.

Lizzie entered the room at the moment, and Mrs. Herrick said to her, —

"George tells me it is his intention to stay with us to-day, if you would like to have him do so, Lizzie. Colonel White not only consents, but advises it."

"O, I thank him most sincerely. I have been

wishing that he would stay. I feel, and *know*, as you
do, that this is my dear mother's last day of suffering.
God's will be done, though my heart break! O, Mrs.
Herrick, will you break the sad tidings to Mary that
another day will see her motherless? I have given her
to understand, for weeks past, that mother could not
live a great while; but I presume she has no idea how
very near the time is at hand; and I don't feel as if I
could tell her."

"I will do it as gently as possible, dear Lizzie,"
replied Mrs. Herrick.

"O, my dear little sister!" continued the grief-
stricken girl. "I will try to do my duty, for her
sake. I *will* do it, with Heaven's help. *No mother —*
sad, sad!"

Ah, yes, sad indeed for two young girls to lose
their mother! And what a responsibility devolved on
Lizzie! Doubting her own ability to walk in the
straight path, she must point the way and guide the
steps of a much younger sister. But she had early
learned to ask counsel of her heavenly Father, and she
would not ask in vain in this instance. So thought
Mrs. Herrick and George, as they listened with admiration to the modest and yet deep resolve of the grief-
stricken orphan girl. Let us hope there is much good
in store for that faithful daughter who has given her

young life-energies so freely, year after year, to her long-suffering mother.

It was a silent and solemn day in that humble dwelling, where the death-angel waited for the dissolution which was to give one more body to the dust, and another soul to the realms of eternal life. There had been no visible change in Mrs. Swift, during the long day, other than a gradual sinking away, which indicated an easy death, probably without again rallying from the nearly unconscious state in which she had continued for many hours. However desirable this might be with regard to the poor suffering woman herself, yet the two young daughters could not but hope that their dear mother would speak their names once more before she passed away forever.

About half an hour before sunset the dying woman seemed wonderfully to revive, and requested to be partially bolstered up by the pillows, and to have the curtain put aside at the window which looked towards the west, by the foot of her bed. When these arrangements were completed, and her children, with Mrs. Herrick and George, stood by her bedside, she smiled and said, —

"How beautiful! *My* sun is setting with the glorious orb of day, to rise again in the morning amid splendor and glory far exceeding those of the natural sun.

14

Death has no terrors for the Christian soul, for Hope and Faith render the passage of the dark Vale clear, safe, and peaceful. And now, my dear children, grieve not uselessly for me when I am gone, but live true Christian lives, trusting to a happy reunion hereafter. Mary, my darling, receive a mother's parting blessing." And with the assistance of Mrs. Herrick she placed her hand upon the head of her little sobbing daughter, saying,—

"My dear child, receive the parting blessing of your dying mother, and may the blessing of Heaven also rest upon you forever."

The dying Christian seemed to gain strength of voice as she pronounced her simple blessing on her latest born; and now, as she fixed her loving eyes upon Lizzie, the faithful, and reached to take her hand, there was a depth, and clearness, and richness in her tones, as she uttered the following words, that struck the ears of the solemn little group of listeners as coming from the already untrammelled soul, rather than from the stiffening lips of death:—

"Lizzie, my dear, kind, self-sacrificing child, I have no earthly riches to bequeath to you, but, instead, I leave to you a dying mother's undying gratitude. And to my own blessing, I feel certain, will be added that far richer one of your heavenly Father, under whose kind protection you are, and will remain forever. Continue your implicit faith and trust in God, and he will raise up friends for you here on earth, and finally receive you in his own abode."

George Herrick stood at one side of the weeping Lizzie, and his mother at the other, while little Mary bowed her head upon the bed in half-stifled sobs. The tears of the mother and son mingled with those of the grief-stricken girls. Mrs. Swift still retained the hand of Lizzie, whilst her eyes seemed to wander from her face to that of the youth at her side. George fixed his gaze upon the face of the dying woman, heaved a long sigh, and then slowly, solemnly, and as gently as if he were about to extend his hand to receive some delicate flower, whose beauty might be shattered by the least rude contact, he raised his right arm and encircled the waist of the young maiden at his side. He uttered not a word, but the movement unmistakably said, "I will shield this dear girl from all harm." The dying woman observed the tender, deep-meaning act, smiled approvingly upon it, uttered feebly, but distinctly, "It is well," and without a single struggle, closed her eyes forever on all earthly scenes.

CHAPTER XX.

THE ORPHANS.

THREE weeks after the death of Mrs. Swift, Lizzie sat in her little work-room with an open letter in her hand, which she had just finished reading for the second time, and seemed to be weighing carefully the contents of the same in her mind.

"He is a dear, kind uncle," she said at last; "but I cannot accept his generous offer. I cannot think of leaving this dear old home; I cannot leave my mother's grave. I should prefer living here by the labor of my own hands, to a life of perfect ease anywhere else;" and she placed the open letter in the hands of her kind companion, Mrs. Herrick, who still remained with the orphan girls while their friends — at the head of whom was Colonel White — were planning their future.

Mrs. Herrick read the epistle attentively, and returned it to Lizzie, remarking, —

"It is truly a letter of great kindness, and the offer your uncle makes you is most generous, and is very creditable to his heart. You ought to weigh the matter well, my dear young friend, before you decide to decline the proposition. You know it embraces Mary as well as yourself."

. " I know it does. Were it not for that, I could not entertain the idea for a moment. But, O, I do want to do that which is for the best for my dear little sister — best for her in every sense of the word."

" Well, Lizzie, you know it is not required of you to decide with regard to the matter immediately. Your uncle very considerately says in his letter that you must take ample time in making up your mind, and that whether you decide to accept his invitation extended to you and Mary to make his house your future home, as members of the family, or remain where you are, he shall be perfectly satisfied, and can never lose sight of, or interest in, one who has devoted years of her young life so faithfully to a sick and long-suffering mother, and that mother his own and only sister. So, dear girl, you must take further time for consideration; and, with the advice of your friends here in town, I have no doubt you will come to such decision as will be the best for both you and Mary."

" My dear uncle is extremely kind to leave me thus free to decide, and yet promise to continue to assist us. I hope my decision will be for the best. But do you know, Mrs. Herrick," said Lizzie, looking up with a half-concealed smile, "that I am exceedingly *self-willed?* Whenever I have to make up my mind about anything, no matter how important it may be, I am very apt to decide at once with regard to it; and, although I am always willing and anxious to listen to the advice of friends on the subject, yet I seldom change my mind. And the probability is now, with regard to the subject of this letter, that I shall adhere to my opinion already expressed; although I will gratefully listen to the good advice of friends."

"So you think you are 'exceedingly self-willed'—do you, Lizzie? Perhaps your friends may have more charity for you than you have for yourself, and apply the term 'decision of character' to that which you call 'self-will.'"

"I fear that my friends are often too indulgent for my own good, dear Mrs. Herrick, and perhaps humor me in my opinions when they are far from being correct."

"No, no, my darling girl; your friends are too sincere to do that. Such a course would not tend towards your true happiness, which they all so much desire. But with regard to your uncle's letter: Colonel White, you know, is coming in this evening, and as you have chosen him your legal guardian, you will, of course, lay the whole matter before him, and ask his advice. *I* have no fears at all about your ' self-will.' "

Early in the evening Colonel White called to see the orphan girls, according to appointment. Lizzie gave him her uncle's letter to read, which led to a full discussion of the whole subject, and, finally, to a settled plan with regard to the future of the two young girls. The colonel manifested no surprise when Lizzie informed him that her preference was to remain in her native village. Indeed, he had expected such a decision, and was well pleased with it. He had opened a correspondence with Mr. Hart, the uncle in Chicago, before the death of Mrs. Swift, and in his last letter to that gentleman, after her decease, he had suggested a plan with regard to the two orphan girls, in case they decided to remain where they were, that their uncle had fully sanctioned in his answer to the colonel, bearing the same date as that of his kind letter to Lizzie, above referred to.

Colonel White now proceeded to lay the whole plan fully before his young friends, in the presence of Mrs. Herrick, leaving them free to decide in the matter without a word of argument on his part. The plan was briefly as follows : —

Lizzie and Mary were to continue to occupy their

own dear home. As it would not be proper, however, for two young girls to live wholly by themselves, the house, excepting one room and bedroom, was to be let to some small, quiet family. The house had been well planned, by Mr. Swift, for six good rooms; but misfortune, sickness, and death had prevented him from carrying out his original intentions, and hence the whole upper part remained in a partially finished state. The little property had been mortgaged, years before, to Squire Belmont. The mortgage had expired, and the right of redemption ceased, long ago; but, fortunately for Mr. Swift and his family, Squire Belmont was not the man to distress a fellow-creature who was struggling against misfortune. Hence the family had never been disturbed, and had continued to live in the house rent free.

Colonel White knew all the circumstances, had talked with the squire about a relinquishment of the claim, had informed Mr. Hart of the very generous terms agreed to by Squire Belmont, and had received instructions from him to secure the property for the orphans, and to have the house finished at once, so as to make it tenantable throughout, — that is, if his nieces decided ·to remain in Harryseekit, — and he would forward a draft to meet all demands. (He had already placed in Colonel White's hands funds sufficient to pay all the bills of Mrs. Swift's sickness since her husband's death, the funeral expenses, and to meet any immediate wants of the orphans.)

When Colonel White had divulged thus much of the proposed arrangements, he waited to see how it would be received by his interested listeners. Lizzie, however, was so much overjoyed at the prospect before them, and so filled with gratitude at the kindness of Colonel White, the generosity of Squire Belmont, and the munificence of her uncle Hart, that she could scarcely articulate, in broken sentences, her hearty approval of the scheme. And although Mary had taken some childish delight in the anticipation of a long journey to see her wealthy relatives, and perhaps to live with them, still, her love for Lizzie, and her confidence in whatever she decided upon, outweighed every other consideration, and caused her to exclaim, —

"O, Lizzie, how nice it will be to live here always!"

"Yes, I would rather live here, where our dear father and mother lived, and sickened, and died, than in a palace at a distance. But," she continued, addressing Colonel White, "*how* are we to live here? What can I do to support myself and Mary, and to keep her at school?" and a shade of concern settled upon the thoughtful girl's handsome face.

The kind old gentleman, however, as he now unfolded the remainder of his plan, soon caused the shadow to pass away, giving place to sunshine and happiness. Mrs. Herrick was a most excellent operator on the sewing machine; and, after Mrs. Swift's death, when she decided to remain for the present with the orphan girls, she had requested George to bring Mrs. White's machine to her there, that she might employ her time advantageously. Lizzie had at once taken an interest in the useful household article, and quite soon convinced Mrs. Herrick that a very little practice would make her a competent operator. This fact had been mentioned to Colonel White, who advised Mrs. Herrick to encourage her young friend in the practice; and now his object in having done so was made manifest. He informed Lizzie that he understood she could work very well, even now, on the sewing machine, and as Mrs. Herrick would remain with her some weeks longer, she could still further perfect herself in that branch of industry. She could then have the free use of the machine just as long as she pleased; for Aunt Betsey had a machine, and they could make that do the work for both families.

"And now," continued the colonel, "for your means

of support. Young Mr. Hunt, who has just opened a
small fancy goods store at the Corner, and was recently
married to Susan Payson, with whom you are well
acquainted, mentioned to me the other day that he
wanted a small house, as they were about to commence
housekeeping. I told him I expected this would be
finished within a few weeks, and that he could probably
have all but two rooms. He said it would be just what
they wanted. And furthermore, when I informed him
that you were learning to work on the sewing machine,
he said he could give you all the work you wanted to
do, if you learned to do it neatly, and would pay you
a *living* price for it. He is an honorable man, and
you can depend upon what he says."

Lizzie was as well pleased with the latter part of
Colonel White's arrangements for their future liveli-
hood as she had been with the former, and longed for
the day to come when she could feel that she was sup-
porting herself and sister by the honest labor of her
own head and hands. She thanked the kind old gentleman over and over again for his fatherly interest in
their welfare, and affectionately pressed both his hands
in hers as she bade him good night.

Turning to Mrs. Herrick, after the colonel left,
Lizzie said, with much earnestness, —

"O, such a man as Colonel White ought to live always!"

"I never knew, I never heard, of his equal," replied Mrs. Herrick. "Every moment of his life seems to be devoted to doing good to his fellow-creatures. You and I, dear Lizzie, should be thankful for such a friend."

"I am truly thankful," responded the young girl, in unmistakable tones of sincerity.

On the very next day following the acceptance of the plan suggested by Colonel White, carpenters were busily at work finishing off the house that had been commenced years before by Mr. Swift. A few weeks sufficed to make it ready for occupancy. Mrs. Herrick returned home, with regrets on both sides, for a sincere and mutual friendship between her and Lizzie Swift had grown stronger and deeper every day they remained under the same roof. Mr. Hunt took possession of his part of the house, and Lizzie took possession of the sewing machine — both well pleased with the premises. Mr. Hunt immediately gave Lizzie some work, and it was done to his entire satisfaction. Whereupon he informed her that he would keep her employed all the time. The young girl was now truly happy. Her household duties were just sufficient to keep her from working too steadily at the machine, and hence, both her health and spirits were kept in a good, sound condition.

When Colonel White called on Squire Belmont with the amount of money (two hundred dollars) which that gentleman had previously named as an equivalent for relinquishing all claim to the Swift property, he could not prevail upon him to accept a single dollar, although he was informed that it had been forwarded by Mr. Hart for that express purpose.

" No," said Squire Belmont, " I cannot take a single mill of that money. I have already attended to the cancellation of the mortgage, and the property now stands free and clear to the heirs of John Swift; and you, colonel, as their legal guardian, must see that it remains so."

" But what about this sum of two hundred dollars?" asked Colonel White.

" It belongs to the two girls. Put it out at interest for them," replied Squire Belmont. " Were it not that this war business has drawn so largely on my purse, I would make it up to five hundred dollars. I consider Lizzie Swift a girl of unequalled goodness, and I should be tempted to dance at her wedding — provided the man should ever be found that is worthy of her."

" I thank you, squire, most sincerely, in the name

of the orphans, and will see that this money is safely invested for them," responded the colonel.

So judiciously did Colonel White manage the affairs for his two young wards, and so liberally did every one holding any claims against the little estate discount in their favor, that he found — after paying every demand, and placing in Lizzie's hands a sum of money sufficient to last them till she should make her first quarterly settlement with Mr. Hunt for rent and work — he should be able to place a little more than three hundred dollars at interest for them.

Lizzie remembered her mother's dying words, "Continue your implicit faith and trust in God, and he will raise up friends for you here on earth," and she determined to abide by that faith.

CHAPTER XXI.

RECEPTION OF GENERAL HOWARD.

LTHOUGH events of vast import to the nation were constantly transpiring on the different battle-fields, which served to inspire the Young Invincibles with a determination to keep up their organization, and to profit by experience, these events are too well known to all classes of readers to need to be chronicled here, even did not our space and object forbid such a course. Indeed, we feel compelled to pass in silence over a twelvemonth, leaving the boys of Harryseekit during this time under the friendly and patriotic instruction of their stanch old friend Colonel White, this long step taking us to the spring of 1863, the commencement of the third year of the rebellion, and well along in the second year of the existence of the Young Invincibles.

" Have you heard anything more about the expected visit of General Howard?" asked Tom Sprightly of his friend George Herrick, at the close of a fine afternoon, as the two lads walked across the corner of the orchard from Mrs. Herrick's to Colonel White's.

"No, nothing positive; but the colonel feels quite certain that he will come," replied George.

"Peppermint and shoestrings!" exclaimed Tom; "I hope he will come. I want to see the one-armed hero."

"I hardly think the general will be very well pleased with his reception, if he is to be treated to ' peppermint and shoestrings,'" said Lucy White, laughingly, as the boys came unexpectedly upon her and Lizzie and Mary Swift, as they turned round the corner of the house. "George tells me he really believes you have given up turning somersets. I give you all credit for that. But please tell us, *Lieutenant* Sprightly, when you are going to give up your ' peppermint and shoestrings'?"

Our friend Tom had been recently promoted.

"About the same time, probably, that some young ladies of my acquaintance give up their ' popped corn,'" replied the newly-made lieutenant, with a low bow.

All three of the girls had their hands full of snow-white corn of Lucy's own preparing, and were gratifying their palates with the delicious morsels.

"Well, that time will soon come," rejoined Lucy.

" for my supply in the ear is getting to be rather short. I really believe that you and George make 'raids' upon it. But come, Lieutenant Tom Sprightly, how much corn shall I give you to abandon your 'peppermint and shoestrings' forever?"

" Give me every particle of corn you hold in your hand," responded Tom, " and I'll bid good by to 'peppermint,' and *throw in* the 'shoestrings,' same as they do down to the Corner when you buy a pair of shoes. Is it a bargain?"

" Yes, it *is* a bargain," said Lucy, approaching quite near to Tom, " if you will faithfully promise to abide by it."

" And you shall have half of mine, also," added Lizzie.

" And I will take a portion of the other half," said George, helping himself very liberally from Lizzie's willing hand.

" And you shall have half of mine, too," joined in Mary, as the three young girls gathered merrily about Tom, who was always ready for a little frolic.

" Now for your promise," said Lucy, as she extended towards him her tempting hand.

" I most faithfully promise," began Tom, assuming a ludicrously sober countenance, " in the presence of these living, *eating* witnesses, that from this hour

15

forward I adopt 'popped corn' in the place of 'peppermint.'"

As Tom completed his "oath of allegiance," more sincere, probably, than many taken in other sections of the country, Lucy restored him to the "rights of citizenship" by emptying the contents of her hand into his — which favor he acknowledged by an immediate gustatory attack upon the dainty "rations."

"Here comes grandfather!" cried Lucy, turning her eyes towards the Corner. "And see, he holds up a letter, and his face is all smiles."

"Just as it always is, bless his dear old soul!" was the exclamation from the admiring Lizzie.

"I know by his looks, Tom, that he has favorable news from General Howard. He expected a letter from Squire Belmont, who is in Boston, with regard to the general's visit. We shall see him, my boy!" and George gave his companion such a slap on the shoulder as caused half the corn in his hand to shower down over his feet.

"Pep — *popped corn* and shoestrings!" exclaimed Tom, as he stooped, and commenced gathering up his treasure, some of which had actually lodged among his shoestrings. "George Herrick, you have crippled me for life! How shall I ever be able to walk with all these *corns* on my toes?" and he began to limp about, amidst the laughter of the girls, as if he had been in reality a fit subject for a chiropodist.

"I beg pardon, Tom," said George, laughing with the rest. "I had no idea that Lucy's corn still possessed such power of 'popping,' or I should have been more careful."

"Well, I'll not quarrel with you in presence of the ladies," replied Tom, with assumed dignity. Then turning towards the girls, he continued, holding up between his thumb and finger one of the largest and whitest of the kernels of corn, "Why is this like your grandfather, Lucy?"

"I'm sure I can't tell," she replied. "I give it up."

"Because it's *kernel all over white;*" and the kernel entered Tom's mouth just at the moment that the colonel entered the gate, amidst the ringing laugh of the little group of young folks assembled near the house.

"I am glad to see that you are having a merry time of it," said Colonel White, as he took an extended hand of Lizzie and Mary in each of his, while Lucy darted in between them to give and receive the usual kiss.

"We were laughing at one of Tom's poor jokes," remarked George, as the colonel looked at him inquiringly.

"And I am appreciating my own joke, which others are not capable of doing," said Tom, as his teeth performed the office of mastication upon the last of Lucy's "supplies."

Lucy repeated the conundrum to her grandfather, who laughed heartily, while he shook his cane at the author of it, and told him he must lay joking aside for a day or two, and remember that he was an officer in the Invincibles, for there was a great honor awaiting that company, and he trusted every member would sustain himself with credit on the occasion.

The colonel then read the letter that he held in his hand, which was from Squire Belmont, and contained the pleasing intelligence that General Howard had fully decided to take Harryseekit in his route, and would arrive there in the morning train of the next day but one.

"And now, George," said the colonel, as he folded the letter, "you and Tom must display what military talent you possess to the best advantage, for the Invincibles must turn out with full ranks, and perform escort duty to the distinguished visitor."

"Bravo!" cried Tom, fairly jumping about for joy. "We can do the business up in good shape — can't we, George?" and he returned the slap upon the shoulder with good interest.

" I think we shall have no reason to be ashamed of our boys," replied George, in a confident tone. "We must notify them all early to-morrow to meet at the armory the next morning at eight o'clock. And we'll have Uncle Bill take hold of the guns and accoutrements to-morrow, with the help of some half-dozen of us boys, and put an extra touch upon them."

Mrs. White had joined the party in front of the house in time to hear the reading of the letter by her husband, and expressed much gratification, with the others, at the expected visit of one of our bravest generals and best of men.

"Lucy, my dear," said. she, " we shall have to stir ourselves to-morrow to put things in proper train for the next day. We couldn't make any great display if we should attempt it; and I have no wish to try; but we must give the general a cordial reception, and a good, substantial dinner."

" O, I dare say the general has eaten many a poorer dinner than you will give him, grandmother," replied Lucy. "But then I'll do my best to help you, for I *should* like to have things in pretty good shape. And Lizzie will come down early to-morrow, and assist you, too, and she will be worth a dozen like me ; and then, with the help of Mrs. Herrick and Aunt Betsey, I shouldn't wonder if we got up a splendid dinner !

You'll come — won't you, Lizzie? and Mary can come right here from school; " and the animated girl looked at her young friend for an answer.

" Yes, indeed, if I can be of the least assistance," was the cheerful reply.

So we see that the fine old lady had the ready promise of willing hands to assist in getting up a " good, substantial dinner" for the general.

The morning and the hour had arrived when General Howard was looked for by the good people of Harryseekit, and the grounds round about the little depot, as well as the street leading from it up into the centre of the village, were filled with highly expectant, though most orderly, citizens. At the end of the platform nearest the street were drawn up the Young Invincibles, now mustering seventy-five muskets, ready to receive the distinguished visitor, and to escort him through the main street to Colonel White's residence.

Directly is heard the familiar " whistle," and in a few moments more the train comes thundering along, and then gradually, as if by instinct, draws up at the little brown depot. The " Christian Hero" stepped upon the platform. No one could be mistaken. There was the solitary left arm. Its mate had been yielded up far away on the battle-field, one of the many sacrifices, in the work of putting down an unrighteous rebellion. The moment his foot touched the platform, cheer upon cheer rent the air, handkerchiefs waved, hats were thrown up, and such demonstrations of enthusiasm manifested for some minutes as were never before witnessed in Harryseekit.

The visitor was accompanied by a single officer of his staff, Major Payson, and Squire Belmont. Colonel White stepped forward and gave the general a cordial greeting. He then introduced him to the selectmen of the town and some of the most prominent citizens. While this was taking place, the assemblage was agreeably surprised by hearing a full band of music strike up "Hail to the Chief!" There was nothing like a "Band" in the town; so, of course, this was unexpected to every one. But Squire Belmont, being aware that good music would add much to the enjoyment of the occasion, had engaged the musicians, at his own expense, at Capeland, where the train had been delayed for half an hour, and brought them on with him. They had left the cars quietly, on the opposite side, at a hint from the squire, and joined the Invincibles, and commenced playing before their presence was known to the crowd generally.

As the band began to play, General Howard turned his eyes in that direction, and noticed for the first time the military company drawn up to receive him. For a moment he fixed his gaze upon the perfectly-formed line, as if surprised at such soldierly bearing, and then, turning to Colonel White, with a smile of satisfaction on his countenance, remarked, —

"Squire Belmont has been giving me a little historical sketch of the 'Young Invincibles,' and I had become somewhat interested in them. I was prepared, however, to see a mere company of boys; but I see a body of *soldiers*. You must have drilled them long and thoroughly, colonel."

"I paid considerable attention to them for the first few months," replied Colonel White; "but since that time they have been drilled almost wholly by their own officers — more especially by their captain."

"And what is the captain's name?" inquired the general, taking out his memorandum-book.

"George Herrick," replied the colonel.

"A good-sounding name," said General Howard, as he wrote it down and returned the book to his pocket.

"And a good, sound young man that bears it," remarked Squire Belmont, with much emphasis.

The carriages which were to convey the general and his friends through the village to Colonel White's residence were waiting on the street, a few rods from the depot, and the party now moved in that direction. As they neared the escort, the order was given, "Present—

arms," and every musket was brought into position at the same instant, almost as if one mind and hand had governed the entire movement.

" Admirable ! " exclaimed the war-worn hero, whose eye was fixed upon the young soldiers.

Having passed along the front of the " Invincibles," Colonel White and his friends conducted their distinguished guest to the carriages in waiting, the military immediately formed and marched to the head, the band struck up, " See, the conquering hero comes ! " and the " procession " commenced its march up the street. And although this procession could not be said to be either extensive or magnificent, yet the general afterwards often referred to his reception at Harryseekit as one of the most gratifying he met with during his brief tour through the state.

Arriving at Colonel White's, the procession halted in front of the gate, over which, extending from the branches of a tree on either side, was a very handsome display of flags which Uncle Bill had managed to arrange, without help from any one, while waiting for the arrival of the guest.

Captain Herrick again formed his company in line, outside the gate, and the general was conducted along their front and into the hospitable dwelling of his patriotic old friend, where he had received many a cordial welcome in earlier years. As he approached the gateway he said, —

" Colonel White, these flags are very tastefully displayed. Who arranged them ? "

" O, that is the work of my old sailor friend, general, while the rest of us have been waiting for you at the depot," replied the colonel.

" Yes, yes ; I remember him. Let me see ; Uncle Bill Ballast — is it not ? " inquired General Howard.

" The same," responded his friend.

" I shall be happy to take the old tar by the hand," rejoined the general. " I love an old sailor next to an old soldier ; " and he pressed Colonel White's arm which was locked in his.

They had now entered the house, where the general was met and warmly welcomed by Mrs. White and Lucy. He was then introduced by the colonel to Mrs. Herrick, as his wife's companion and Captain Herrick's mother, to Lizzie and Mary Swift, as his wards, and to a few of the neighbors who were present by request, — not forgetting Uncle Bill, whose native bashfulness soon gave way before the free and cordial manner of the great and good soldier. The general congratulated Mrs. Herrick upon having so promising a son, saying he had taken much interest in him, said a few pleasant words to the two sisters as to their good fortune in

being under such excellent guardianship, and then
turned to Uncle Bill, with an allusion to the navy,
to the hardships and bravery of the sailors, to their
undying love and veneration of the old flag, and then
complimented the old seaman personally for his despatch and taste in arranging the bunting so gracefully
over the gateway.

The old sailor was fairly delighted at this compliment from the great general, but was not a little
puzzled to know how to acknowledge it. However,
he thought some reply was due, and he must " heave
ahead."

" You see, general," commenced Uncle Bill, " it's
very little that a stiff old chap like me can do, any
way. But I *do* love to handle the ' stars and stripes ! '
Why, sir, a man that can't work the flags of his country into something beautiful *ain't got any soul !* I've
seen the time when I could make those two trees out
there look like a commodore's ship just after a great
victory ! But those days are past now, and I'm about
the same as laid up in ordinary," continued the old
sailor, descending again into the self-deprecating tone
and manner in which he had commenced. " Besides,
I never *could* do much ashore. The land is all well
enough, I s'pose, in its way ; but then there's nothing
like a good ship and plenty of sea-room. A chap

knows what he is about then, if he only keeps his reck'ning."

"I rather think you will have to make up your mind to spend the rest of your days on shore, though," responded the general, smiling at the old sailor's love and preference for his former vocation.

"O, yes, sir; I made up my mind to that, long ago. And I'm anchored here in a first-rate harbor," rejoined Uncle Bill, in a more contented tone.

"You have a very fine parade here in front of your house, Colonel White," remarked the general, looking from the window; "and I see that Captain Herrick is about to improve it. Really, it affords me great pleasure to look at those youthful soldiers. Come, I must have a nearer view;" and passing out at the door, he walked rapidly down to the gate, followed by the whole party.

George Herrick, as we have found on various occasions, was a cool, clear-headed youth, and he was in nowise embarrassed when he became aware that the movements of his company were to be closely observed by a general right from the battle-field. In fact, his confidence grew stronger as the responsibilities of his position increased. And the result was, that he drilled and manœuvred his company for the space of twenty or twenty-five minutes with such perfect ease and accuracy as to call forth many expressions of warm commendation from the general and Major Payson.

Finally, as the company marched up near to the gate, and was ordered to a rest, General Howard at once advanced and shook Captain Herrick warmly by the hand, complimenting him as to his efficiency as a commander, and congratulating him upon the perfect discipline and martial appearance of those under his command. After an introduction to Lieutenants Sprightly and Sherman, the general addressed a few words of encouragement to the company, praising them for their military proficiency, and thanking them for their attentions to himself.

He hoped, he said, that the terrible war in which the country was engaged would terminate before they were old enough to be called to the field; but, if such proved to be the fact, they must not feel that their time and labor in bringing themselves to such perfection in soldierly bearing had been wasted — far from it. They had set an example worthy to be followed by the rising generation throughout the length and breadth of the country. An interested, *patriotic* " citizen soldiery " would be one of the future safeguards of this blessed Union saved.

" I am highly gratified that this opportunity has

been afforded me of witnessing the proficiency of the Invincibles," continued the general, " and I shall often revert to this occasion with pleasure and pride. And now, my young soldier boys, I propose three rousing cheers for Colonel White, the originator of your organization, and your early instructor and constant friend, whose *patriotism at home* has done so much to warm the hearts and nerve the arms of our brave soldiers in the field."

And immediately the air resounded with the proposed cheers — not only by the " Invincibles," but by the collected multitude all around — with an earnestness which showed that they came from the heart. Colonel White stepped forward and bowed his acknowledgments, and then proposed, —

" ' Three times three ' for our brave General Howard."

Again the cheers pealed forth with increased energy, and for a few moments the scene was one of almost wild enthusiasm. As the excitement died away, the general briefly thanked the citizens of Harryseekit for their kind reception, expressed his fullest confidence in the integrity and strength of the administration, and told them that patience and patriotism for a year or two longer would place the Union on a firmer base than ever before.

Colonel White and his guests now returned to the house, the band played several lively airs, Captain Herrick dismissed his company, and the crowd quietly dispersed in different directions — all highly delighted with the proceedings of the morning.

CHAPTER XXII.

THE "LAUNCHING."

SOON after entering the house, Colonel White said, —

"General Howard, we have been building a fine, large ship at the Point, and she is to be launched at two o'clock to-day. How would you like to take a ride down there and see her go off?"

"Nothing would suit me better," replied the general. "I always thought it a scene of grandeur to see a ship move swiftly and gracefully into her proper element; and years have elapsed since an opportunity of the kind has presented itself. I will certainly go to the 'launching' — that is, if we can return in season for me to take the five o'clock train this afternoon."

"There will be ample time," responded the colonel, "if you and the rest of the gentlemen have no objection to a twelve o'clock dinner; for it would be too late to dine after our return."

"I breakfasted early this morning, as is my custom,"

rejoined the general, "and an early dinner will suit me all the better. In fact, I never adopt 'fashionable hours,' unless they are forced upon me."

Major Payson, Squire Belmont, the "town authorities," and the remainder of the party, numbering twelve in all, were unanimous for the early dinner and the "launching," and the colonel at once informed his wife and Mrs. Herrick of the decision. Now, if Mrs. White and her friend had not been sensible women, this piece of information — requiring dinner two hours earlier than had been at first intended — would have put them into a complete "flurry." As it was, they quietly informed the girls of the new arrangement, and all hands set at once to work with the determination of having dinner ready at the appointed time.

It is true, Lucy was a little nervous, at first, for fear all their arrangements could not be properly carried out; but the assurances of her grandmother and Mrs. Herrick, together with the confident words and manner of Lizzie Swift, soon restored her equanimity, and matters went on bravely in that happy old family kitchen.

The subject of the "launching" was again referred to in the parlor, and the colonel said to General Howard,—

"I am about to commit to your charge a little secret, general. You are aware that it is the custom,

16

in these parts at least, to paint the name of a new vessel on her stern, a day or two before the time of launching, and cover it immediately with canvas, which is only removed, and the name pronounced, at the moment the vessel glides into the water. Were the custom different, and the name not already painted, I should be pleased to give you the privilege of christening the ship. But, as it is, I think we have selected a name which you will honor. We call her the 'General Grant.'"

"The very name, of all others, I would myself have selected," replied the general, in an animated tone. "I do indeed honor that name."

General Grant was at this time on his famous march "to Vicksburg," and the public had just begun to realize, in a degree, that he possessed military genius of a high order.

"I believe that General Grant will prove himself to be a great captain," said the colonel. "I have unbounded confidence in his military ability."

"And so have I," was the response of General Howard. "He is *the* general of our day; and the people and the government will very soon acknowledge it. Vicksburg is sure to fall before him, and then he will be called to confront Lee in Virginia; and when he once sets himself down before Richmond, no earthly power can cause him to turn back until his object is accomplished. Mark my words, gentlemen," continued the general, becoming unusually earnest in his manner, " Robert E. Lee will, sooner or later, surrender his boasted Army of Virginia to Ulysses S. Grant."

At precisely twelve o'clock dinner was announced, and the party at once repaired to the well-laden board. Whether all the preparations had resulted in such an entertainment as Lucy had been pleased in anticipation to style " *splendid,*" we shall leave for that young lady to decide ; but that it fully came up to the more sensible idea, put forth by her venerable grandmother, of " a good, substantial dinner," was sufficiently well attested by those whose good fortune allowed them to partake of it.

Dinner over, the gentlemen took seats in their carriages, and were soon on their way to the Point. The road was in excellent order, and the drive a very pleasant one, and " Dancing Jim," who had the honor of drawing the chaise which contained General Howard and Colonel White, was not backward in showing his spirit and speed. The general remarked upon the fine qualities of the horse, which led his owner to relate the little adventure he met with on that road five years previous, on which occasion George Herrick was first brought to his notice. He was warm in his praises of

George, not only on the occasion alluded to, but during the whole five succeeding years.

Among other things, the colonel stated that he had never known the youth to have the slightest difficulty with any other boy, though every one knew him to be as brave as a lion. He then alluded to the strong friendship existing between George and Tom, to the many good qualities of the latter, notwithstanding his propensity for fun and frolic, and wound up his commendation of the two lads by saying that he believed both of them, if they lived to be men, would make their mark in the world.

"Really, Colonel White, you interest me more and more in young Herrick," said the general. "Take care, or you may lose him. I shall be tempted to speak a good word for him in a high quarter."

"I should be loath to lose him," replied the old gentleman; "but if it were for his own and his country's good, I should not regret it."

The conversation on the subject was here brought to a close by the sudden halt of Dancing Jim at his usual stopping-place under the shed by the entrance to the shipyard, where the rest of the party soon made their appearance, and all walked down to the ship together.

There was a numerous concourse of people present, among whom were George Herrick and Tom Sprightly,

with many other members of the " Invincibles," and
scores of the younger class from the village, all of
whom had started early and walked the whole distance.
The crowd was unusually large — some having come
to see the "launching," while many others came to
see the general, the news that he was to honor the
occasion with his presence having rapidly spread
through the town.

All was hurry and bustle among the workmen. It
was within a few minutes of the time appointed for
the ship to speed her course down the slippery ways.
A large number of spectators had been admitted on
board, and the steps were removed to prevent her deck
from being dangerously crowded ; and already the fast-
falling blows from the carpenters' stalwart arms, all
along the ship's keel on either side, told that the
" wedging-up " was going on in earnest. Presently
there is barely a perceptible start of the huge hulk ;
then all is still. Again, a few rapid blows ; another
start. The crowd on her deck all jump and stamp ;
the jar increases her motion. Quick — swift — like
lightning the ship glides down the well-greased ways,
ploughs deep into the briny element, as if happy in the
opportunity thus to lave her long-seasoned sides, rolls
a huge wave on before her, and, in another moment,

the " General Grant " floats upon the water almost as lightly and gracefully as a swan !

Now go up the long, loud cheers from the workmen and spectators on the shore, which are heartily answered from the crowded deck of the ship. Then came the usual trial to ascertain whether the vessel was " crank " or " stiff," by all on board stationing themselves along the deck on one side from bow to stern, and quickly rushing across to the other side, then back again, and so to and fro for a number of times, rocking the ship like a cradle. The " launching " was a complete success, and the " General Grant " was pronounced to be " A, No. 1."

In a few minutes the ship was hauled in to the little wharf, near the yard, and her passengers scrambled ashore. As soon as the decks were cleared, Colonel White invited General Howard and the gentlemen accompanying him on board, to examine the inside finish of the vessel, which had been most thoroughly and superbly accomplished. In fact, she was a ship worthy of her name. While this examination is progressing, we will go with the crowd to a field just across the road from the shipyard, to finish up the sports of the day with a wrestling match — an invariable custom on a launching day at Harryseekit.

CHAPTER XXIII.

THE WRESTLING MATCH.

HE manner of wrestling on the present occasion was to be that variously styled " square-hold," "arms'-length," " toe-to-toe," &c. ; that is, the two wrestlers stand face to face, each with his right hand hold of his opponent's left shoulder, and his left hand grasping tightly the right elbow. Thus firmly grappled, each endeavors to throw the other upon his back by dexterously tripping at his antagonist's feet, and at the same moment suddenly exerting the strength of his hands and arms in the opposite direction. The rules of the contest prohibit the use of the arms without the accompanying " trip," because such a course would invariably give the stronger party the advantage. There is a good deal of skill to be displayed in this mode of wrestling, and it is not always the stronger one of the two that comes off as conqueror.

A ring was soon formed, and two boys, about twelve

years of age, were speedily contending for the victory.
The first fair throw decided the question in this case,
when the vanquished party or his friends at once
selected another champion to fill his place. Thus the
match went on, the contestants gradually increasing in
size and years.

Finally, Tom Sprightly was brought into the ring.
Tom was considered the smartest wrestler of his age
in the whole town, and his back seldom, if ever,
touched the ground until some one of a man's size
and powers was matched against him, who would at
last cause him to yield under a great disparity of
weight and strength.

On the present occasion it seemed as if Tom was
to stand the champion of the ring to the last, for he
had thrown all those of his own age who would
wrestle, and a number that were two or three years
his seniors. At length a great strapping fellow, named
Jack Dunham, twenty years of age, weighing one
hundred and eighty pounds, was brought forward.
The best of good nature had prevailed throughout,
and as Tom now stepped forward to the unequal
contest, he laughingly said, —

" Don't fall on me too heavily, Jack."

" I make no promises," replied the burly fellow,

who was something of a bully, and inclined to be quarrelsome.

At this moment, and before the wrestlers had taken hold of each other, George Herrick stepped quickly up to his young friend, and laying his hand on his shoulder, said, in a low, earnest tone, —

"Tom, you had better not wrestle with Jack. You know you threw him about a year ago — and he has never forgiven you. He has threatened since then, that if ever he got hold of you again he would break some of your bones."

"O," replied Tom, in the same confidential tone, "I guess he didn't mean anything. He always *talks* big. I want to straighten him out just once, George."

"I'm afraid you'll be sorry for it, Tom."

"Come, George Herrick, what are *you* interfering for?" said Jack Dunham, impatiently. "Are you afraid your baby will get hurt?"

"I think Tom has wrestled enough for one day," replied George, very calmly, "and I advise him to stop."

"Perhaps *you'd* like to take his place," sneered Jack.

"No; I never wrestle," responded George.

"And I'll wrestle but this once more to-day," said Tom, as he stepped forward and took hold of his powerful opponent.

Contrary to all rule, Jack at once commenced twitching Tom violently about, wholly by the strength of his arms, fairly lifting him clear from the ground, and then endeavoring suddenly to dash him prostrate upon his back. But all to no purpose, for Tom was sure to baffle every such attempt by coming down fair and square upon his feet. Some of the spectators expostulated with Jack about his unfairness; but he gave no heed to their remonstrances. Finally, having become pretty thoroughly tired out by his great exertions, he desisted for a moment to take breath, and allowed his arms to relax. Quick as thought his wiry antagonist sprang in upon him, tripped him, threw him flat upon his back, and instantly jumped out of his reach.

The shout that went up from the excited and highly-gratified crowd could have been heard a mile away. The vanquished wrestler jumped to his feet, showing much passion, and, with an oath, sprang towards Tom. But George Herrick, who had feared some trouble from the moment Jack Dunham was brought into the ring, threw himself directly in front of the advancing bully, and, taking his young friend by the shoulder, said, almost authoritatively, —

" Tom, we must leave."

" No, you don't," said Jack; and he attempted to place his powerful hand on George's shoulder.

George, however, jumped quickly to one side, and, pushing Tom before him, was in another instant well in among the crowd. All this was the work of a moment, and before any one could interfere. George very well knew that Tom had many more friends present than Jack could claim, and was not at all fearful that he would get hurt; but he thought the surest way of preventing a row was to take his young friend out of the way.

" Come back, you cowardly sneaks ! " shouted Dunham.

But the two lads continued to move farther away.

" George Herrick ! " continued Jack, " come back yourself and wrestle, if you're afraid to let Tom come."

" I have told you that I never wrestle," replied George, very calmly.

" Come back and fight me, then," roared the bully, urged on by a few of his own clique.

" I have less inclination to fight than to wrestle," rejoined George Herrick, with perfect good nature.

" You're cowardly dogs ! " again shouted the quarrelsome fellow. " I should like no better fun than to thrash you both at once."

" But that would not be very good fun for *us*," responded George, still in pleasant humor.

" You are the most contemptible, cowardly, sneak-
ing puppy I ever saw, George Herrick," almost
screamed young Dunham, maddened beyond measure
by the other's perfect coolness.

" *I* can't stand this any longer," said Tom. " Let's
go back."

" No, no," replied George. " It is better to take no
notice of the blackguard's words."

" Say, Herrick," once more called out Jack, being
determined to provoke George to anger by some
means, " are you bound to California to look up
that nice father of yours that ran away because your
mother was no better than she should be ? "

" Shame ! " " Shame ! " " Shame ! " resounded all
around, in tones that indicated no good to young
Dunham. But, in an instant, George Herrick was
seen, with a face of frightful paleness, tearing his way
through the crowd like a roused lion, with Tom closely
following, towards the low, mean fellow who had
uttered the insult to his mother's name. Confronting
the bully, with his lips almost touching his face,
George spoke in subdued, deliberate, and measured
accents, that seemed to be the very embodiment of
deep passion under the control of a resolute and
powerful will : —

" Jack Dunham, you might have continued to heap

epithets upon *me* until you were gray, without moving my anger in the least; but listen: — When I was twelve years old I promised my mother, if I lived, I would be her protector. Now, detestable blackguard that you are, you must instantly apologize for the insult you have offered, or, by the sacredness of that promise, I will tear the confession from your foul throat."

There was a terrible earnestness in the youth's words and manner; but young Dunham was a fighting character, and being three years older, and some fifty pounds heavier, than George Herrick, he felt confident of an easy victory over him, and consequently replied, contemptuously, —

"Apologize to you, boy? I'll give you an apology that you won't forget in a hurry;" and he sprang upon and grappled his lighter antagonist with a might that seemed to threaten almost instant annihilation. George's friends trembled for his safety, as they saw him thus in the grasp of the stalwart bully. But it was at once evident that George Herrick's close and compact form contained a muscular power and a nervous elasticity that would prove a full equivalent for the other's superior size, and slower, though greater, strength. After a moment or two of fierce struggle, locked tightly in each other's arms, George suddenly

lifted his burly antagonist from his feet, gave him a
quick whirl, and brought him to his back on the
ground with such force as nearly drove the breath
from his body, and caused him to break the bear-like
hug with which he had enclosed him in the first
grapple.

Quick as thought George now planted one knee
upon his fallen foe's breast, crowded his left hand hard
upon his throat, and, with his right arm uplifted, again
called upon him to take back the insulting words. But
Jack had caught sight of the end of his antagonist's
neck-tie, which was a strong, double, black ribbon, put
loosely round his neck, and clutching it with both
hands, he began twisting it violently. George felt the
band rapidly tightening about his throat, and endeavored to unclinch the fellow's fingers; but they were as
firm as the jaws of a vice. George was beginning to
turn purple in the face. The bystanders now discovered how matters stood, and thought it time to interfere. But Tom Sprightly was the first to spring to
the rescue, exclaiming, —

" The villain will strangle him ! "

George Herrick, however, had not lost his remarkable presence of mind, nor his power of action. He
had thrust one hand again upon Jack's throat, to see
what effect that would have, and with the other he

motioned Tom away, for he could not speak. Then instantly clapping his hand into his vest pocket, he took out his knife, opened it with his teeth, slipped it down the back of his neck, and cut the ribbon in two — though it was girted in so closely that he cut the skin as well. He was now free, and jumped quickly to his feet, leaving his severed neck-tie in the hands of his baffled enemy.

' Jack also sprang to his feet, and the two stood again face to face, looking each other unflinchingly in the eye. In the aspect of George were plainly written the unbending determination and undying resolve to "fight it out on this line if it takes all summer," while on the part of the other was manifest a brute stubbornness, mingled with towering passion and burning shame, which evidently sought deep revenge. As George closed his knife, and returned it leisurely to his pocket, while the blood was seen slowly trickling round on either side of his neck from the slight wound he had given himself, he said to his antagonist, in his usual calm and deliberate way, —

" Jack Dunham, I should prefer that this unhappy affair might end just where it is. One word from you will do it. Take back the insulting language."

" Never ! " was the dogged reply.

" Then, by the fair fame of that dear mother whom

you have so grossly vilified," rejoined George, in low, deep tones, " I will grind the confession from your lubberly bones."

He made a step or two backwards, caught the front parts of his loose sack-coat in either hand, and threw both arms back in the act of slipping it from his shoulders, as he had found it in his way during the previous contest. His unprincipled antagonist, who had been waiting for an advantage, instantly sprang forward, and attempted to deal George a heavy blow in the face while his arms were thus entangled in his coat. But at the moment the blow was about to fall, Jack found both his arms brought suddenly to his sides from behind, and pinioned there as if by bands of un-yielding iron. Colonel White's son Mark, a man in the prime of life, standing six feet two, and stout in proportion, had seen the cowardly movement in season to spring forward and wind his powerful arms around young Dunham.

" Coward, as well as blackguard and bully ! " exclaimed Mark White, as he held the young man as powerless as an infant. " Were it not for the satisfaction of seeing George Herrick punish you as you deserve, which I know full well he *will* do, I would give you one such hug as would bring all your ribs together, and press the very breath from your body."

THE BULLY PUNISHED. — Page 257.

George had freed himself of his coat, and rolled his shirt-sleeves above his elbows, exposing an arm that called forth remark from all that stood near him, for it seemed to be a compact mass of nerve and sinew.

" There, go — and meet your reward," continued Mr. White, releasing young Dunham from his close confinement. " George, don't spare the detestable cub ! "

But George Herrick was reasonable to the last. Once more he proposed terms of peace.

" Jack, will you recant ? "

" No, fool ! " and again he sprang forward to the conflict.

This time, however, George was prepared for him, and he was met with a quick, powerful blow between the eyes, that sent him reeling and staggering back, and would have caused the bully to measure his length upon the ground, had not his few friends gathered up so near as to save him from the fall.

" At him again, Jack," they cried. " Give him one of your ' settlers.' "

But the fellow's brain was evidently a little bewildered. Perhaps he had a confused idea that he had been kicked by a horse, and needed a few moments' time to measure the distance between his head and the horse's heels, for he did not respond very readily to his

17

friends' urgent appeals. George did not follow up the advantage he had gained, disdaining anything like unfairness even to an unfair foe, but stood calmly awaiting the enemy's next move, whatever it might be.

During this momentary cessation of hostilities, some one shouted from the roadside near by, —

" George! George Herrick! Is it possible that is you? Come here — quick! "

George knew the voice well without even turning.

" Ask your father to excuse me a few minutes longer," said he to Mark White, as that gentleman started for the road.

" Stick to your job, George, and finish it up," replied Mr. White. " I will explain matters to father and his friends."

It was but a few steps to the fence, and as Mr. White reached it, he found his father, who had driven close up to it, leaning forward from the chaise, and still calling and gesticulating earnestly to George Herrick.

" Don't get excited, father," said Mark. " George is doing well enough."

" Doing well enough! " repeated the old gentleman, excitedly; " what do you mean? Here I have been praising him to General Howard all day, and among other things, have said that I never knew him to quarrel with any other boy; and here we find him, with the words of praise scarcely cold from my lips, engaged in a disgraceful fight." The colonel spoke in a tone partaking both of grief and bitterness.

" Yes, it is a disgraceful fight," replied his son ; " but the disgrace is wholly on one side. Father, you would have *caned* young Dunham yourself, old and forgiving as you are, if you had heard the insulting puppy ; " and, in few words, he related the facts of the case.

" I knew the provocation must have been very great," rejoined Colonel White. ". Really, I can't blame George."

" Blame him ! " responded General Howard, " who *could* blame him? He is fighting in the defence of his mother, as you and I have fought in the defence of our country. He that would flinch in the one case would be certain to prove craven in the other."

All eyes were now directed to the combatants, as the contest seemed about to be renewed. Jack Dunham was far from being subdued. The well-directed blow he had received produced a stunning effect for a minute or two ; but he thought too much of his reputation as a great fighter to entertain for a moment the idea of yielding to a lad three years his junior and of fifty pounds less weight.

"Once more, and for the last time, Jack Dunham, will you recall the words you have spoken?" asked George, still willing to end the contest without more blows.

"I tell you, *No!*" roared the bully. "Do you think I am a little boy, to give up for a single chance blow?"

"Then I will make the shortest possible work of it," cried the other; and not waiting to act on the defensive this time, he leaped in between Jack's long, powerful arms, and dealt him another of those short, quick blows — seemingly from a wonderful spring in the elbow — that laid him his length on the ground. Then jumping upon his prostrate form, he punished him so severely that he was soon obliged to cry for quarter.

"Enough! enough! Let me up!" he bellowed.

"That won't do," returned George, determinedly. "You must apologize for that base insinuation, or I will hold you here fast till the crows pick the bones of both of us."

"I was wrong," cried the now completely subdued bully. "I take back what I said about your mother."

"All right," said George. "I ask nothing more;" and jumping to his feet, he slipped on his coat, which

Tom Sprightly was holding, and quickly made his way, without exchanging a word with any one, to Colonel White's carriage.

"Have I done wrong?" he asked, as he grasped the colonel's hand, which was extended to him.

"I am sorry that the circumstances required you to punish the vulgar fellow," replied the old gentleman; "but — but — but *I'm glad you did it!*"

George's countenance brightened a little.

"And what will my mother say about the affair, think you?"

"She will thank Heaven for having so brave a defender," promptly replied General Howard. "I can answer for her. — Come, jump right into the chaise. We can make room for a 'conqueror' — can't we, colonel?"

"By all means," replied the old gentleman, "if you desire it. — Come, George, jump in."

"I thank you, gentlemen, but you will please excuse me, for my clothing is somewhat bloody from this scratch on my neck. Besides, my friend Tom, here, expects my company home. I think I will walk."

"Well, then," said General Howard, warmly grasping the youth's hand, "I will bid you good by, hoping we may soon meet again. Do not let this personal encounter, which you could not honorably avoid, mar the pleasurable recollections of this otherwise happy day. I shall long remember the enjoyment of these few hours spent in Harryseekit; and to your conduct, *throughout*, I am indebted for much of that enjoyment. Farewell."

The brave soldier and Christian gentleman was obliged to hurry away to the railroad station, for five o'clock was drawing near. The crowd dispersed, and George and Tom walked leisurely homeward. But all the wit and humor of the latter could not remove the oppression that weighed upon his companion's mind. It was his first combat, and though in a just cause, still he sincerely hoped it might be his last. No one, however, can read futurity.

When George reached home, his mother threw her arms about his neck, exclaiming, —

" My dear boy, Colonel White has told me all. You need not say one word about it, for I know it would be unpleasant to you ; " and she kissed, with affection and pride, the high, broad forehead of her young and brave defender.

" Was Lizzie Swift present when Colonel White related the unhappy occurrence ? " asked George.

" She was."

" And what did she say ? "

" 'Mrs. Herrick, you have a noble protector in George.' "

" Mother, the recollection of the affair has weighed heavily upon me all the way home. But I will try to forget it."

Had Lizzie's words removed part of the weight?

CHAPTER XXIV.

CRAZY PHILIP.

HE first time that Jack Dunham showed himself at the Corner after the day that he received his well-merited chastisement at the hands of George Herrick, he was encountered and severely talked to by Philip Dillaway, a man subject to frequent fits of insanity, but who, on this occasion, was perfectly sane.

He met young Dunham in the public square of the village, and seizing him by the collar, with an iron grasp, he held him securely for the space of fifteen or twenty minutes, and lectured him in a manner that called forth shouts of approbation from all who heard him, whilst the severity of his language was such as to cause the young bully fairly to wince under its scathing effect. He finally wound up by telling Jack, if he dared to show himself again at the Corner, he would not escape the next time with mere words, as he would have him arrested and sent to prison as an i/ ., quarrelsome vagabond.

Jack was so much alarmed at the threats uttered by Philip Dillaway — fearing, undoubtedly, that when one of his crazy fits came upon him he might do him some great bodily injury — that he left the village that very night, for parts unknown, under circumstances to be hereafter related.

The good citizens of Harryseekit were very much surprised at the severity and length of the reproof given to young Dunham by Crazy Philip, because it was so contrary to his usual custom. For years he had been extremely taciturn when in his right mind, scarcely ever speaking to any one unless he was first spoken to, and seeming to labor under continual de-. pression of spirits on account of his great misfortune.

But Philip had good reasons for entertaining the best of feelings towards Colonel White and his family, and he was particularly friendly to Mrs. Herrick and George, both of whom had ever treated him with the greatest kindness and delicacy on account of his terrible affliction. Hence, when he heard of the insulting language made use of by Jack Dunham concerning Mrs. Herrick, and of his forcing George into a quarrel with him, it aroused his indignation to such an extent as to cause him to break through his usual reserve, in the manner stated, in defence of his friends; and he proved himself to be a most effective champion in this case, as he fairly frightened the low, quarrelsome fellow out of the place.

Philip Dillaway, or " Crazy Philip," was one of those unfortunate beings, frequently met with in a community, who are deprived of reason by the heavy hand of disease. He was at this time about thirty-five years of age, and had been subject to periods of lunacy for more than ten years. He was remarkably bright when a boy, and an excellent scholar. Before he was twenty, he was engaged as teacher of one of the village schools, which situation he continued to hold, year after year, until violent convulsive fits became so frequent with him as to render it wholly unsafe to retain him any longer in that responsible situation.

These fits increased in frequency and violence until it was noticed that the young man's reason was slightly affected for a day or two after the convulsions passed away; and then he would seem to be in the perfect possession of all his faculties until again stricken down by another fit. But these terrible convulsions finally proved too much for the unfortunate young man's reason; and on a still Sabbath morning in the month of June, just as the village bell was calling the good people to their places of worship, Main Street, on which the Dillaway family lived, was thrown into great commotion by Philip, who was seen rushing through the street, without coat or hat, pointing and looking up to the heavens, shouting loud and wildly as he ran, and quoting passages from the twelfth chapter of Revelation, concerning the doings of the "Great Red Dragon." Women and children fled, screaming, in all directions; but the crazy man made no attempt to molest any one, until some of the men in the street, seeing his father and two younger brothers in pursuit, attempted to stop him, when he scattered them as if they had been men of straw, and continued on his way. The crowd increased both in his front and rear, and numerous attempts were made by powerful men to arrest his course; but, with a giant's strength, he knocked them this way and that, as if they had been mere toys, and continued his career.

Finally, two or three strong men came up behind him, and grappled him at the same moment, and succeeded in detaining him till more help reached them, when, by overwhelming weight and numbers, the poor lunatic was dragged to the ground, secured hand and foot by ropes, and borne bodily back to his home, ragged, bruised, and bloody, still shouting passages of Scripture, and followed by his poor old mother, crying and begging of the men to be careful not to hurt her poor, unfortunate boy.

On reaching the house, he was secured in a strong, old-fashioned arm-chair; and the doctor, being called in, succeeded in opening a vein in his arm, by which means his strength was soon reduced, and he became more quiet; but his friends did not dare to release him for a number of days, until they were fully convinced that he was perfectly sane.

The next month, and the next, similar scenes were enacted — the poor maniac inflicting and receiving much bodily injury. Colonel White endeavored to impress upon Philip's own folks and their neighbors, at the outset, that they were pursuing the wrong course. He insisted that they should humor his whims as far as practicable; that he would, if not opposed, do nothing more than run up and down the street and shout his Scripture texts; that if allowed to have his own way, so long as he molested no one, he would much sooner become calm; and that all the cruelty necessitated by the present course would be thus avoided.

Philip was a great reader of the Bible, and when his crazy fits were upon him he used Bible language pretty much altogether — sometimes quoting verse after verse, at other times repeating over and over again the same verse, and again making some single clause answer his whole purpose.

It was not long before Colonel White had an opportunity to test his theory with regard to the management of Crazy Philip. On his way down to the Corner one day, when near Mr. Dillaway's house, he saw Philip in the street, running up and down, shouting lustily, with a crowd of men closing in around him preparatory to seizing and securing him. In this instance he did not seem inclined to run away, but would seize first one and then another by the arm, as if he wished them to accompany him somewhere. As the colonel drew nearer, he understood the lunatic's shout, which was — "Compel them to come in! — Compel them to come in!"

Colonel White walked directly up to the crazy man, who instantly seized him by the arm, shouting, "Compel them to come in!" Instead of struggling, as others had done, to get away from him, the colonel yielded at once, saying, "Yes, Philip, I will come in with you;" and immediately walked along with him towards the house.

"Compel them to come in!" repeated the lunatic, looking over his shoulder at the crowd in the street.

"Follow us into the house," said the old gentleman to the neighbors; and they all complied immediately.

As soon as Philip saw that the crowd was following, he smiled, and said, —

" The wedding is ready, but they which were bidden were not worthy."

" So you wanted to 'compel them to come in' to the wedding — did you, Philip?" inquired Colonel White.

" Go ye therefore into the highways, and as many as ye shall find, bid to the marriage," was the scriptural reply of Crazy Philip, as they all entered the house. The lunatic was now apparently calm, and, having accomplished his object of procuring guests to the imaginary wedding, he appeared perfectly satisfied. Looking around the room, with a smile upon his countenance, he continued, —

" So those servants went out into the highways, and gathered together all, as many as they found, both bad and good; and the wedding was furnished with guests."

There was no more trouble with Philip on that occasion, and consequently all were convinced that Colonel White had the right idea as to the proper manner of treating him. This humane system was adopted; and in less than a year there was scarcely a child in the village that entertained any fear of Crazy Philip, whereas the whole neighborhood had been subjected to a state of terror during all the time that the harsh and cruel treatment was continued.

And thus the poor lunatic had gone on, year after year, for ten long years, up to the present time, his crazy fits occurring once a month, and usually continuing four or five days in succession; but he had never injured any human being after his friends adopted Colonel White's humane recommendation.

He would neither eat nor sleep in any house, however, during his terms of insanity. His mother soon discovered that he entered the house in the night time, and took away food; and a particular door was ever after left in such a way that he could enter and leave the house at pleasure. During his crazy freaks he often wandered to the woods, where he would remain several days at a time, visiting his father's house at night for food; and when his insane fits subsided, he invariably returned to his home and his bed while the family slept.

CHAPTER XXV.

" FIRE! FIRE!! FIRE!!!"

HE evening of the day on which Philip Dillaway so severely lectured Jack Dunham for
his gross insult to the fair fame of Mrs.
Herrick, and for his unprovoked attack upon George,
was occupied by the latter and his friend Tom, up
to a late hour, in talking over the somewhat exciting events of the past few days, and finally by settling down upon Crazy Philip's strange encounter with
Jack in the village square.

" It seems so queer that Phil should take it into
his head to lecture Jack!" said Tom, in reply to a
remark by George. " I really believe he must have
been about half crazy, or he never would have talked
so long as he did to-day. It's about time for him
to have one of his wild freaks."

" Crazy or not," responded George, " he gave Jack
a first-rate dressing down, and I hope it will do him
good."

"I think *your* 'dressing down' will do him the most good," said Tom, dryly.

"I don't know about that, Tom. As a general thing, I believe fighting has a bad effect upon all concerned."

"Perhaps you don't believe in fighting the *rebels*, Mr. Non-resistant?"

"The country was obliged to take up arms, in self-defence," replied George.

"And *you* were obliged to take up 'fisticuffs' in defence of your mother. O, George, I wish *I* had a mother to fight for! But as I have not, I will yet fight for my country."

"Not for the *sake* of fighting, though, Tom, but for the justness of the cause — I know your heart well enough for that, my boy;" and George noticed a tear in his companion's eye.

Our two stanch young friends said good night, and as the village clock tolled off the hour of eleven, Tom started for home, leaving George to bestow himself quietly in bed, where he was soon fast asleep, the evening having been spent in his bedroom. When Tom was about half way home, he met Philip Dillaway on the run. His mutterings to himself told the youth that his crazy fit was upon him.

"Why, Philip, where are you going at this time

18

of night?" said Tom. "Come, go back home with me — won't you?"

The crazy man dashed to the opposite side of the street, exclaiming, —

"Flee from the wrath to come! Flee from the wrath to come!"

Tom knew it was useless, as well as dangerous, to attempt any force in the case, and as the unfortunate lunatic kept on his way up the street, the lad continued his walk homeward, and a few minutes more found him in bed. He felt little inclination to sleep, however. His thoughts seemed determined to follow Crazy Philip.

Some few minutes before twelve 'o'clock, George Herrick was suddenly aroused from his sound sleep by a loud knocking upon his bedroom door, accompanied by Uncle Bill's well-known voice, —

"Turn out — quick, George, quick! The colonel's barn is all in a blaze!"

The youth was wide awake in a moment. He sprang from the bed, slipped on his pants, stuck his feet into his slippers, and caught his cap from its usual hook in the entry as he rushed along and out at the back door.

"Fire! fire!! fire!!!" he cried, at the top of his lungs, as he ran across the corner of the orchard, leaving Uncle Bill to finish the work of arousing the inmates of both houses.

George was the first to reach the barn. The fire had already burst through the roof at the eastern corner, and he saw at a glance that the building could not be saved. Picking up a stone, at a single blow he shivered the padlock that fastened the door at the side of the barn where the horses and cow were kept, and instantly drove the latter into the yard. Returning, he led Old Noll to a place of safety, and then ran back for Dancing Jim. Loosing the halter, and speaking soothingly to the young horse, George endeavored to lead him from the burning building. But the place was now oppressively hot, and full of fierce, bright flame. The animal snorted, held back, reared and plunged, but absolutely refused to leave his perilous position.

Colonel White, Uncle Bill, and a few of the nearest neighbors were now on the ground, and the colonel called loudly to George to come out of the dangerous building, and leave the horse to his fate.

"In a moment," said George; and seizing a small horse-blanket that was at hand, he threw it over the animal's head in such a manner as to completely shield his eyes from the dazzling light of the fire, passed the halter round it to keep it in place, spoke

a few gentle words to the now quiet horse, and led
him out into the open air without further difficulty.

"George," said the colonel, "your presence of
mind has saved Dancing Jim's life. I shall not forget it."

But it was no time for a reply from George, for
the fire was rapidly shooting forth its forked tongues
along the dry, shingled roof of the barn, towards the
carriage-house and wood-shed, which connected with
the dwelling-house, and if the wind should spring up
from the north or east, the latter building, even,
could scarcely be saved. There were now, probably,
twenty-five men and boys assembled at the fire, Tom
Sprightly being one of the number, his sleepless mood
and nimble feet having enabled him to be among the
first from any considerable distance who reached the
scene.

There was a fire-engine at the Corner; but as
nearly all the regular firemen had long since enlisted
for the war, there was some considerable delay before the machine reached the scene of the conflagra-
tion. In the mean time the neighbors worked with
a will. There was not one among the number who
was not ready to risk life and limb, if necessary, in
behalf of Colonel White.

The colonel was remarkably cool and collected, and

gave directions with regard to the management of the fire with calmness and good judgment. The barn was connected with the carriage-house by a broad, wooden platform, extending to the second story of the latter building, with a door at either end, and being sufficiently elevated for a large gate to swing beneath it. No attempt was made to save the barn; its destruction was inevitable; but before the fire extended to that portion of it nearest the other building, this large gate and platform were pulled down and wholly cleared away.

Tom Sprightly, who was as sure-footed as a cat, now mounted the roof of the carriage-house, and spread blankets and woollen carpets, which were passed up to him, over the entire end of the building nearest the fire; and these being kept continually saturated with water from the never-failing well close at hand, together with the fact that the slight air stirring was from a favorable quarter, fortunately confined the fire to the barn itself. And when the engine finally arrived, the building was a heap of ruins; but further danger was at an end.

Soon after Tom ascended the roof, and commenced his dangerous labors, he cried out, —

"Some of you see who this fellow is skulking among the apple trees!" He indicated the direction.

George Herrick and two or three others instantly rushed through the gateway between the fire and the carriage-house, and were just in season to see Crazy Philip running with the speed of a race-horse across the lower part of the orchard, in the direction of the bridge, and to hear, in his peculiar tones, —

"The young Philistine came with his midnight torch to consume the house of the righteous! He shall be pursued even unto the ends of the earth, and destroyed totally!"

Pursuit was considered useless; and as George and his companions returned, and reported what they had seen and heard, many believed, and some few said, that Crazy Philip must have set fire to the barn. Colonel White, however, would not for a moment entertain such a thought. He would as soon believe, he said, that one of his own family had been guilty of the deed.

The engine had now been playing with good effect for some little time upon the smouldering ruins, and there seemed to be not much more work for willing hands to do. George and Tom, with two or three other members of the Invincibles, had volunteered to keep guard over the premises till daylight, and the neighbors were about to disperse, after having received the hearty thanks of the colonel and his family, when Mark White drove up to the house, his horse fairly reeking from hard driving. He lived at a distance of three miles from his father's. A fire was an unusual occurrence in Harryseekit, and hence people came from remote parts of the town to ascertain who the sufferers were. Mr. White was confident, soon after leaving home, that the fire was near his father's house. Consequently he spared not his horse.

"Well, father, so the old barn is gone," said Mark, as he grasped the old gentleman's hand; "but we should be thankful the fire was no more disastrous. When I was on Beech Hill I thought house, barn, and all were in flames."

"Yes, Mark, we have much to be thankful for," replied the colonel. "The barn was an old companion of mine, it is true, and I shall miss it; but then it gives me an opportunity to build a better one for somebody's benefit."

"Have you any clew to the origin of the fire?" inquired the son.

"It is all a mystery," the old gentleman answered.

Tom Sprightly now mentioned the circumstance of his having met Crazy Philip when he was on his way home from Mrs. Herrick's, and George related what he and others had seen and heard in the orchard.

Mark White was then asked if he thought the unfortunate maniac was the author of the fire.

" No, no," replied that gentleman, emphatically. "But let me tell you whom I think I have seen since I left home. Just this side of Beech Hill I met some one on the full run who looked *precisely* like Jack Dunham. Not fifty rods behind him came Crazy Philip, dashing over the road at his greatest speed, and crying out as he ran, 'The young Philistine shall be pursued to the ends of the earth.'"

"Are you *sure*, Mark, it was Jack Dunham?" asked Colonel White.

"No, father; I am only *sure* it looked precisely like him. I should not be much afraid, however, to take my oath that it was he."

"Strange!" mused the old gentleman.

Taking all the circumstances into consideration, it is not at all surprising that the suspicion was transferred from the poor lunatic to the unprincipled bully, nor that the theory was at once entertained that Philip had been keeping watch upon Jack's movements, and although not in season to prevent him from burning the barn, that he had followed up his impressive lecture by driving the incendiary from the place.

The kind neighbors now returned to their homes,

George and his companions kept up a faithful watch, and all was quiet in Harryseekit for the remainder of the night.

The very next day Colonel White commenced preparations for rebuilding his barn, and pushed the work ahead with his characteristic energy. After the usual lapse of time, Crazy Philip returned to his home; but if he knew aught of Jack Dunham's whereabouts, the secret remained securely locked in his own breast.

CHAPTER XXVI.

THE INVINCIBLES SHOW FIGHT.

S the spring of 1863 advanced, the patriotic Young Invincibles became more and more interested in their military exercises, feeling a laudable pride in the compliments so lately passed upon their organization by the war-worn General Howard. They had recently taken up target shooting, which added not a little zest to their weekly parades. These were really spirited affairs, as there was much good-natured competition for the " best shot." The firing was, as a whole, very clever, while some few of the Invincibles were pronounced *first-rate* marksmen by those competent to judge. But George Herrick's unflinching eye and steady nerves were always sure to bear away the palm — except on some particular occasions when Uncle Bill favored them with a shot. He had been unanimously voted an honorary member, and nothing suited the boys any better than when they could persuade the kind-hearted old sailor to join them in their exercise of target-shooting.

Uncle Bill was a remarkable "shot." He could place the ball within a quarter of an inch of any given point in a succession of a dozen shots, without a single failure. George Herrick was no less pleased than the company in general at such times as the old seaman favored them with his accurate skill in firing, notwithstanding he knew for a certainty that on all such occasions his own shots would rank only second best. George had a twofold object in view in thus willingly submitting to Uncle Bill's superiority in target practice —.he knew it was slightly gratifying to the company at large to see the old sailor deprive him of a portion of his easily-earned honors, and his generous disposition prompted him to yield with a good grace ; then, again, he was well aware that these trials of skill with a superior marksman were just the lessons he required to perfect him in the practice ; and George Herrick's ambition was to *excel* in whatever was worth attempting at all.

As the Invincibles marched up the road from their target ground, late on a Wednesday afternoon, on which occasion the firing had been unusually good all round, they noticed, when they halted in front of Colonel White's, that a Mr. Rogers, from the Lower

Landing, was standing at that gentleman's door in earnest conversation with Mrs. White, for the colonel was absent with Squire Belmont on that day, attending to some business in the county town. The moment the company halted, the lady beckoned George and Uncle Bill to come to her — which summons they obeyed without a moment's delay.

After a conference of five minutes, the old sailor was seen to proceed to the stable, and George Herrick returned to his company.

"Boys," said he, as soon as he came within speaking distance, " you can probably have an opportunity to-night, if you wish, to try your hand at ' *rebel* ' targets. You know the pirate Tacony has been all along the coast here for a few days past, destroying our fishing vessels and coasters; and last night she captured and burned the ' Water-witch,' owned in this town, and sent the crew off in the small boat, who succeeded in landing near Turnville, about twenty-five miles up the bay from here. A son of Mr. Rogers was on board the Water-witch; and as soon as he reached the shore, he sent a telegram to his father concerning the affair, and also stated that they overheard some of the pirates talking about a fine new ship in harbor some twenty-five miles down the bay, which they intended to steal or ·burn to-night, as the case might be, by sending in a boat's crew for the purpose. They undoubtedly meant the ' General Grant.' Shall *we* protect that fine ship, and give the ' rebs ' a warm reception ? "

" Yes, yes, yes ! " was the unanimous response.

" Very well," continued the young commander. " But, boys, I have no right to lead you on any such expedition as this, until you consult your parents. Therefore I shall now dismiss you ; and as many of you as gain your parents' consent may report here to Lieutenant Sprightly at seven o'clock this evening. Request all your folks to keep the matter quiet — and be sure that your cartridge-boxes are well supplied with *ball cartridges.*"

The boys, under a good deal of excitement, scampered off at once towards their respective homes, whilst George Herrick turned to his right-hand man, Tom Sprightly, and communicated to him his plan of operations, as far as formed in his own mind. It was briefly this : George was to proceed at once with Uncle Bill and Mr. Rogers to the shipyard at the Point, where the General Grant still remained at the little wharf, and communicate with the shipkeeper on board, and take advantage of what little daylight would remain for the furtherance of their enterprise. Tom was to take command of whatever number of Invincibles reported to him, and march after dark, by the back road, in order to keep the matter as quiet as possible, to the expected scene of action.

In the course of a few minutes Dancing Jim was taking George and his two older companions rapidly over the road he. had so frequently travelled to the shipyard.

" I wish Colonel White had been at home," said George, slackening the lines a little, as an intimation to Dancing Jim that there was no objection to his doing his best; " for I feel that I am taking a good deal of responsibility in this matter."

" Nonsense," replied Uncle Bill. " If the colonel had been at home, the first thing he would have done would be to turn to you and say, ' George, what had we better do?' Haven't I seen him often enough to know?"

" True, the colonel sometimes asks my opinion," rejoined George ; " but then he always has the best of advice to give on all subjects, and I always feel *certain* I am right when acting under that advice. However, it would not do to delay in this case, and I shall do the best I can."

" And that will be the best that anybody could do," replied Mr. Rogers, who had been a witness to George's remarkable coolness and firmness in his recent severe encounter with young Dunham.

The ship General Grant had been sold to government, and was then in charge of a government officer, awaiting the arrival of a master and crew to take her to New York. This fact was not known to Mr. Rogers. Hence his visit to Colonel White's. George Herrick, however, knew that the sale had been made, and probably he felt the responsibility of his present undertaking to be greater than he would have done if the ship had still remained private property, and Colonel White had continued the principal owner of her. But, fortunately, our young Invincible reasoned from the *war* stand-point — Rescue and preserve everything possible, up to the Union itself, and talk about nice legal and constitutional points afterwards. Waging *war* on a *peace* basis results in the predicament of the man who allowed himself to be run down by a runaway horse on a bridge, because he persisted in adhering to the well-known law, " Keep to the right."

Arriving at the Point, the party proceeded at once to the ship, and communicated to the keeper all the information they possessed with regard to the expected visit from the pirates, offering to stand by the ship with him. George Herrick then informed him that not only were his own services at his command, but he felt confident that a considerable number of his company would be on the spot early in the evening; and although they were boys, he was not afraid to say that they knew how to handle a musket.

Mr. Rice, the ship-keeper, was a patriotic, resolute man, and he at once decided to defend his government's property to the last. He accepted the offer of assistance with many thanks. They immediately held a consultation as to the best steps to be adopted. The little harbor, at the head of which were the shipyard and the small wharf where the vessel lay, is formed by three distinct points of land; two of which jut out a short distance into the bay, converging at their extreme ends to within half a mile of each other, while the third, much less in extent, merely serves to divide the harbor itself into two coves — one of considerable surface, but shallow water, and the other, termed the "*Inner Harbor*," of much greater depth, but not more than an eighth of a mile from the little point up to head water, and a mere stone's throw across from the point to the opposite shore. Here, however, is the channel, with sufficient depth of water at full tide for the largest merchant ship; and here, of course, is the shipyard.

Stretching directly across from the two outer points, are a small, round island, of some half dozen acres, and two rough ledges, the latter being nearly covered at high water. The distances between the southern point and the island, between the island and the southernmost ledge, between the two ledges themselves, as well as between the most northerly ledge and the other point, are about equally divided, thus leaving four narrow passages into the harbor for vessels of light draught at high tide ; but the channel lies between the island and one of the ledges, where there is sufficient depth of water for the largest ship that floats. To appearance, however, there is no safe entrance to the harbor, and no seaman would venture in with his vessel for the first time without a pilot.

The three men had given their views quite freely as to the best course to be pursued in case the pirates did pay them a visit, and some of the recommendations of each had been adopted, and the consummation of a plan seemed near at hand, when Uncle Bill said, —

" Come, George, now for your opinion — you're cap'n, you know."

The other two men also urged George to give his views without restraint.

" Well, I like your plan as far as it goes," said the youth ; " but you propose only to defend the ship. I think we should try and do something more than that — and I believe we can. The Tacony, of course, will

19

not venture into the harbor. There would be danger
of her getting aground on the ledges, if nothing more,
as they can have no pilot that is acquainted with the
various crooks and turns. They will send merely a
boat's crew; not over ten or twelve at most; and if
their object is to burn the ship, probably not more than
half that number will make their appearance. Now,
if my boys come in such force as I think they will, *we
ought to be able to capture every pirate that ventures into
the Inner Harbor.*"

George spoke with such earnest confidence that his
older companions supposed he must have some plan of
operations matured in his mind, and Mr. Rice asked
him in what manner he thought the pirates could be
taken.

" I think we can count upon seeing thirty of our
boys here at least, all well armed, and I would divide
them into three equal squads — one to remain concealed on the deck of the ship, with a boat alongside,
with strict orders not to fire until the pirates had approached to within half gunshot range ; a second squad
should drop down in a boat and land on Eden Point,
concealing the boat with seaweed, and themselves
among the rocks ; while the third party should also
take a boat and land on the other side of the harbor,
directly opposite the Point, concealing themselves and

boat in like manner. The pirates are to be allowed to pass up the harbor unmolested, and when sufficiently near the ship they should be hailed, to make it certain they are enemies, when, if their answers or their actions are not satisfactory, one half of the boys should take good aim and fire, immediately reloading, while the others reserve their fire in case the pirates should attempt to board, or to give them another peppering as they turn to escape, which is more likely to be the case."

Uncle Bill could contain himself no longer, but, springing to his feet, exclaimed, —

" I see it all ! — George, you ought to be a commodore ! "

" The plan looks well, so far," said Mr. Rice, evidently well pleased both with the clear-headed youth before him, and the suggestions he was making. " Come, give us the rest of it as quick as possible, and then let us prepare to put it in execution. — How does it strike you, Rogers ? "

" Capitally ! I believe I'm in for it. Go on, young man."

" Uncle Bill," said George, " you say you ' see it all.' Just give the rest of the plan yourself. If you understand it, you can convey as much in a dozen words as I can in a hundred."

"Ay, ay," responded the old sailor, all animation, as a sort of miniature sea-fight floated before his mind's vision; "it's all plain as day. The firing abpard the General Grant is to be the signal for the other two squads of boys to take to their boats and move steadily up the harbor, while those on board the ship are to take to their boat and follow the pirates down; thus fairly surrounding them, and obliging them to surrender as sure as fate. George, you ought to be a commodore!" and Uncle Bill brought his ponderous fist down on his young friend's shoulder with a force that would have caused a less hardy and well-knit frame to wince with pain.

"You do ' see it all,' " said the youth, smiling.

The three men heartily indorsed George's recommendations, and proceeded at once to make preparations for carrying out the programme. There were a large number of boats about the harbor, so that there was no difficulty in selecting such as were suitable for the occasion. Three of them were brought to the ship's side, and properly furnished with oars, boat-hooks, lines, and whatever else was thought to be necessary for the enterprise. It would be high tide a short time before twelve o'clock; and it was reasonably supposed that the pirates would make their appearance, if at all, not far from that time, especially if they had any idea of getting the ship out of the harbor, as they could then take advantage of the turn of the tide, which would be of no slight assistance to them.

The party on board the ship had completed all necessary arrangements, as far as they were able to do for the present, and now anxiously awaited the arrival of the young soldiers. A short time before nine o'clock they made their appearance, and their young commander was highly gratified as he counted their thirty-six muskets. The plan of operations was speedily made known to Lieutenant Sprightly and his party, who entered into the spirit of the affair with an earnestness that promised success. There continued to be frequent arrivals at the shipyard for an hour after the appearance of the Invincibles, notwithstanding George's precautions, as, in many instances, the citizens had allowed their boys to join the movement only after having decided to be present themselves.

CHAPTER XXVII.

THE PIRATE TACONY.

A T ten o'clock everything was quiet, strict con-
cealment and perfect silence having been impressed upon every one.   Twelve of the young
soldiers were stationed on board the ship, under command of Lieutenant Sherman ; an equal number, commanded by Lieutenant Sprightly, entered one of the
boats, the boat being under the charge of Uncle Bill,
and rowed quietly to Eden Point ; while the remaining
twelve, under Captain Herrick, with Mr. Rogers acting as boatman, silently moved down to their allotted
place on the shore opposite the Point.   The boats were
completely concealed, and not a human being was to
be seen or heard in the vicinity of the harbor outside
of the respective squads of anxious watchers.

No work was going on in the shipyard at this time ;
but the men from the village, some twenty in number,
who had assembled during the evening, were concealed
in the yard, with two large boats in readiness to be

manned immediately if their services should be required; but it was understood by all that George Herrick had planned the enterprise, and was at the head of it, and that his orders .were to be obeyed. Some doubted whether any pirates would make their appearance; but those who knew young Rogers best, believed he had good grounds for sending the information which he had communicated to his father.

It was a clear, starlight night, and sharp eyes could see quite distinctly down to the mouth of the harbor; but although many pairs of such eyes were directed to the different entrances, nothing that looked like a boat had made its appearance up to eleven o'clock. A few minutes after that hour, however, all were surprised to see the Tacony herself heave in sight between Niggerhead Island and the ledge, and sail slowly along so close to the island shore as to make it appear certain that some person must be on the pirate vessel's deck who knew well the depth of water at that place, or they would not have ventured so near the land. Passing a short distance inside the ledges, the vessel dropped anchor, and swung so near to the island that she would scarcely have been noticed except by those who had seen her in motion.

In the course of a few minutes a boat was seen to leave the vessel's side and move along near the ledges,

stretching across the mouth of the harbor until it was
some little distance up into the larger cove, and then
changed its course and made for Eden's Point. By
this movement the boat was concealed from the observation of any one at the head of the harbor until after
it should round the Point. As it neared the spot where
Tom Sprightly and his squad were concealed, ten men
could be distinctly counted as making up the crew ; and
they passed so close to the boys that the latter could
hardly refrain from giving them a shot.

"Shall we pepper them?" whispered one of the
most impatient.

"Obey orders," was the low, prompt reply of
Lieutenant Sprightly.

The pirates used muffled oars, and their boat glided
on with scarcely a sound. After passing round the
Point, the men lay on their oars for a minute or two,
as if listening, peering up the harbor the while, and
then moved on as before. As soon as the strange boat
was far enough from the boys to make it safe to do so,
the squad on either shore removed the seaweed from
their respective boats, and placed them where they
could be launched at a moment's notice. By hugging
the shores closely when they should begin to move up
the harbor, they could not possibly be seen from the
pirate vessel.

Notwithstanding the new and exciting situation in which the Invincibles were placed, they all maintained the most perfect quiet, obeyed orders to the letter, and watched with much anxiety the advance of the pirate boat towards the General Grant. In fact, they almost began to fear that their companions on board the ship did not see the approach of the enemy, so near did they appear to be to the ship's side. The next moment, however, " Boat — ahoy ! " floated down on the gentle evening breeze to the ears of the watchful squads on the shores, as Mr. Rice hailed the pirate crew. The almost instantaneous reply to the hail was a musket shot from the boat; but the keeper of the ship was in a place of safety, and the ball whistled harmlessly over his head.

" Ready — aim — fire ! " shouted Lieutenant Sherman, and six muskets from the ship's deck sent their contents into the midst of the advancing pirates.

This was a reception wholly unexpected by the rascals, as they had reckoned only on finding the keeper on board, and hoped that their single shot had silenced him. The shots from the ship had evidently taken effect, for all was confusion on board the boat, and commingled groans and oaths were distinctly heard by the party on shipboard. Lieutenant Sherman waited long enough to see that the boat had put about for the purpose of retreating, when he again gave the order, —

" Ready — aim — fire ! " and the bullets from the remaining six muskets hastened the movements of the retreating enemy.

The next instant a signal rocket was sent up from the boat, and was immediately answered by a corresponding one from the Tacony.   In one minute's time, the vessel had weighed anchor, and was hastening out past the island into the bay, fearing, probably, that heavier guns might be brought into play.   In the mean time the two squads of Invincibles under Captain Herrick and Lieutenant Sprightly had launched their boats, and were moving steadily and silently up the little harbor, keeping so close to the shores that they had as yet avoided the notice of the Tacony's boat, while the party under Lieutenant Sherman had speedily reloaded, embarked in their boat, and were in full pursuit of the retreating pirates.

As soon as the men concealed in the shipyard were satisfied that the strangers were retreating, they embarked, and pulled out a little distance into the stream, — one boat taking position about midway between the centre of the harbor and the western shore, while the other occupied a corresponding position on the eastern side, — thus guarding against the possibility of escape by the pirates in either of these directions, which they might probably attempt when they should find their retreat cut off by the two boats of Invincibles at the narrow passage between the Point and the western shore. These men had full confidence in George Herrick and the plot he had devised for the capture of the rebel crew, and were determined that the boys should have all the glory of the affair to themselves, unless it became absolutely necessary for them to lend their aid; still they thought it to be their duty to take these precautionary steps.

The pirates seemed to be aware of no other enemy, as yet, than the boat's crew from the ship, which were hotly pursuing them, and were even now near enough to have delivered an effective fire; but such were not the orders. The fugitives were rapidly nearing the narrowest part of the passage, when a few strong pulls brought the two boats lying in wait for them almost athwart either bow, and twenty-four muskets were instantly brought to bear upon them in such close proximity as jeopardized every life in the boat, while Uncle Bill, in stentorian voice, cried out, —

"Tacony boat, ahoy! Heave to, and surrender instantly, or we'll blow you all to pieces!"

The pirates were evidently taken aback. They hastily cast their eyes astern, and saw that the pursuing boat was close upon them; and as they had already tasted fire from that direction, they at once decided that escape or resistance was out of the question; so they determined upon a parley.

" You'll have to suffer for this unprovoked attack upon distressed seamen," commenced the pirate who seemed to be in command of the boat, in answer to Uncle Bill's demand. " We belong to a Union vessel short of water, and have put in here for a supply, and you fire upon us without a word of warning, and treat us as if we were pirates. Now, the best thing you can do is to let us go on board our vessel, and we'll call it all a mistake."

" Tell that to the marines ! " thundered Uncle Bill; " *I* happen to be an old sailor. ' Unprovoked attack upon *distressed* seamen,' eh? You cowardly lubbers, didn't you fire the first shot yourselves? — (same as you did at Sumter) — and now, as then, you beg to be ' let alone ' ! We know just who you are; so you needn't trouble yourselves with any more *yarns*."

" Ready — aim ! " cried the captain of the Invincibles, now assuming the command that properly belonged to him.

" Ready — aim ! " promptly repeated Lieutenant Sprightly.

" Ready — aim ! " was reiterated by Lieutenant

Sherman, whose boat was now sufficiently near to perform its allotted part in the manœuvre.

"Do you surrender, without more words?" demanded Captain Herrick, in a tone that plainly indicated a firmness at the bottom of it that would not bear trifling with.

"Yes — we surrender," was the muttered reply, coming from more than one pair of lips.

"Very well," rejoined the young captain. "Deposit your arms, *of every description*, in the stern of your boat, and then all come forward. Lieutenant Sherman," continued the speaker, "advance, and see that the order is complied with to the letter, and shoot every man who disobeys it."

The lieutenant's boat advanced, and the arms were secured without difficulty, the pirates finding they had a resolute enemy to deal with. The other two parties simultaneously advanced to the bows of the rebel boat, and then, for the first time, the pirates became aware that they had been captured by *a company of boys!* But it was too late now to think of resistance, and they could only growl low curses on their ill luck, as they submitted one by one to the humiliating process of having their hands firmly lashed behind them by Uncle Bill, who had brought some strong small line for that purpose from the ship.

It was found that two of the men were slightly wounded — one in the arm, and the other in the cheek. One stout young fellow among the gang appeared to wish to avoid observation, as he kept his collar turned up about his neck, and had a handkerchief tied around the lower part of his face, although the evening was so mild and warm that such protection seemed wholly unnecessary.

When the pirates were all securely bound, Uncle Bill and Mr. Rogers took seats at the rebel oars, while George Herrick's boat led the way up the harbor, followed by the other three — that of the prisoners occupying a central position. As soon as the men who had acted as a reserve force ascertained that their services would not be required in the capture of the pirates, they had landed, and proceeded on board the General Grant, where they were joined by a considerable number of the neighbors about the Point. And now, as the young Invincibles drew near to the ship, they were met with almost deafening cheers from her deck.

The moment George Herrick's boat reached the ship, he mounted her side, and held a few minutes' conversation with Mr. Rice.

" What do you propose to do with your prisoners?" he asked of George, after heartily congratulating him on the entire success of his enterprise. "Probably you will march them over to the Corner without delay?"

"No; I think that scarcely advisable," replied the young man. "I believe the ship will be the best and safest quarters for them to-night. I propose, with your approval, to place them between decks, with a guard of my boys over them till morning. Besides, the ship cannot be said to be wholly out of danger yet. The pirate may send a second and stronger party to see what has become of the first, or even attempt a rescue, and fire the ship, after all. I intend to stand guard here till morning, when, you say, the master and crew are expected."

Not only Mr. Rice, but all who heard George's opinion, gave assent to the weight of it; and he was urged to go ahead and finish up the work he had planned and carried forward so judiciously thus far. So the prisoners were brought on deck, preparatory to their temporary imprisonment; and as the stout young man already alluded to as wishing to avoid scrutiny jumped from the ship's railing to the deck, the pocket-handkerchief which had concealed his features became loosened, and dropped over his shoulders. Tom Sprightly was the first to notice it, when he suddenly exclaimed, —

" George — look! look! Here is an old friend of yours, turned up *pirate!* "

George, and others, did look, and, to their astonishment, there stood *Jack Dunham*.

" O, this is too bad! " said George Herrick, in a grieved tone. " I would not have believed this, even of *Jack*. To think that any one who is a native of Harryseekit could join with rebel pirates is almost too much to believe! "

The pirates were soon secure between decks, Jack among the rest, who had maintained a stubborn silence throughout the whole affair. It was subsequently ascertained that he had fallen in with the pirates up the bay, in some of their furtive visits to the shore, and had been readily induced, by a small bribe from them and his hatred to Colonel White on account of his great friendship for George, to pilot the expedition into the harbor for the purpose of stealing or burning the General Grant, which he supposed was still owned by the colonel. But whether he was guilty or not of having set the fire that consumed Colonel White's barn, was never known beyond the strong circumstantial evidence in the case.

After Uncle Bill had dressed the wounds of the two sailors, which proved to be slight, and a suitable guard was placed over the pirates, the young captain despatched Lieutenant Sprightly with a squad of eight of the boys down the western shore far enough to ascertain whether the Tacony had actually taken her departure, or was concealed behind the island, waiting to learn the fate of the boat's crew, or perhaps make a second attack upon the General Grant.

Within an hour the party returned, and reported the Tacony under sail some two or three miles down the bay. This relieved the minds of all from any great fears of another attack ; but still a reliable watch was kept up until daylight. Before sunrise the prisoners were brought on deck, some breakfast given them, and then, under guard of their boy captors, were put on the march for the village. The news of the affair had spread, and all along the road the Invincibles were cheered most heartily. They reached the railroad depot just as the morning train arrived from the east, bringing, among others, Colonel White and Squire Belmont, who had been detained over night away from home.

As the train stopped here for wood and water, it gave time for the night's adventure to be related to the passengers, who united with the citizens in bestowing hearty cheers and praises upon our young citizen soldiers. Squire Belmont wrote a hasty note to Collector Jewell, at Capeland, with regard to the matter, and

20

gave it to the conductor of the train, who would be relieved when the cars reached that place. The train moved on, and the Invincibles continued their march up through the village to the gun-house, exciting cheers greeting them the whole distance, where the prisoners were temporarily lodged to await orders from Cape-land, the boy soldiers still standing guard.

Within two hours a special train arrived from Cape-land, bringing the United States marshal and his deputies, who relieved our young soldiers of their charge. The marshal complimented the Invincibles handsomely for their military achievement, thanked them in the name of the government for the good service they had rendered, and promised that they should be reported favorably to the war department.

The prisoners were now brought out, their rope fastenings exchanged for handcuffs, and the whole of them — Jack Dunham the most despised of all — marched down to the depot and taken to Capeland, where they were safely lodged in the fort down the harbor, to await the orders of the government. The Invincibles then marched to their little armory and deposited their muskets, where they were joined by Colonel White and Squire Belmont, both full of praises to the boys for their good night's work. The latter gentleman advised them to go home and rest, take a nap, ask their parents for the remainder of the day as a holiday, and assemble again on their parade-ground at six o'clock that evening, as the colonel and he wished to meet them at that hour for the purpose of a little friendly chat. The boys promised to be on hand at the appointed time, and then departed to their respective homes, really feeling the need of the rest recommended by their good friend the squire, after the arduous and effective duties of the preceding night.

CHAPTER XXVIII.

CONCLUSION.

AT the appointed hour and usual place the Invincibles assembled in full numbers, but without arms or equipments, as they entertained no fears of meeting rebel pirates, or any other enemy, on this occasion, although they were wholly in the dark as to the nature of the "chat" hinted at by their friends. However, they were always quite ready to comply with any expressed wish of Colonel White or Squire Belmont, to whom they felt themselves to be deeply indebted for much good advice and many substantial favors. They felt assured, furthermore, that by becoming a party to the proposed "chat," the time thus spent would be turned to some good account.

Those members of the company who had taken no part in the adventure of the previous night could not but feel some degree of chagrin at what they considered a loss of individual honor. As they consisted altogether of the younger portion of the Invincibles, however, and as it was well understood that they had been restrained by their parents, their feelings were conciliated as far as possible, rather than tantalized, by their companions who had more directly reaped the honors.

This generous conduct on the part of the older boys, together with the pride they all felt individually in whatever conferred honor upon the company as a whole, quickly dispelled the slight mortification that was at first manifested by some of the more sensitive of the younger members as they assembled on this occasion. George Herrick had always mildly censured everything that had an appearance of personal pique or ill will in one member towards another, and as the whole company almost idolized their noble young captain, it was seldom, if ever, that other than the best of understanding existed among them. And this was one great secret of their improvement and success; for we have the very highest authority for the assertion that "a house divided against itself shall not stand" — and the application holds equally good with regard to a company of boys as to a union of states.

The Invincibles did not wait many moments for their two worthy patrons, both of whom were gen-

tlemen of promptness, whether their appointments
were made with boys, for a mere social gathering,
or with men, in matters of the utmost importance.
They advanced and greeted the company, and then
Squire Belmont said, —

"My brave boys: When I requested you to assemble here this evening, it was simply for the purpose
of giving Colonel White and myself an opportunity to
say a few encouraging words to you with regard to
the advancement you have made in military exercises,
and to offer you a slight testimonial of the appreci-
ation in which we hold the services you rendered the
country by your prompt and energetic action last
night. But my pleasure has been greatly enhanced,
as undoubtedly yours will be, by an acknowledgment from a high quarter of those same services.
The promptness of the acknowledgment is evidence
of the importance attached to the matter, and shows
that government recognizes and appreciates every loyal
blow struck for the Union. By this afternoon's mail
from Capeland, I received a brief note from Collector Jewell, enclosing a telegram from Washington,
which he was instructed to forward to the parties
immediately interested. If such is the desire of the
company, it will afford me much pleasure to read
the despatch."

It is scarcely necessary to say that such was the *unanimous* wish. The squire then proceeded to read the following : —

TREASURY DEPARTMENT,
WASHINGTON, —— —, 1863.

MR. JEWELL :

Your despatch, giving information of the attempt to capture or burn the new government ship General Grant, at Harryseekit, is received. Please tender the sincere thanks of this department, of the government, and of the whole loyal country to that brave company of boys, the "Young Invincibles," for their noble defence of the ship, and the capture of the pirates. The name of the young commander, who planned and executed the enterprise so successfully, has been enrolled on the list of those who have distinguished themselves in their country's behalf.

The secretary of war says, hold the prisoners for future action.

CHASE.

" Bravo ! " cried Uncle Bill, who was an interested listener. " George, didn't I *tell* you that you ought to be a commodore?"

" Three rousing cheers for Secretary Chase ! " cried a dozen voices at the same moment.

The cheers were most heartily given. Squire Belmont then proceeded to say, —

"Now, boys, as you have had the *glory*, I will hasten to the *substantial* part of the object in calling you together. The selectmen, and other prominent citizens, are of opinion, after the high-handed attempt of the pirates last night, that we require a 'Home Guard,' and that you have shown yourselves fully competent to act as such. I made the suggestion to the fathers of the town, that, in consideration of your services last night, and for what you may be called upon to do in the future, you were justly entitled to some remuneration; and as I have noticed that your uniforms are becoming a little rusty, and that some of you look as if you had *marched a trifle too far through your pantaloons*, I proposed that the town should furnish you with a new uniform. The proposition was favorably received; but the appropriation will have to be made by vote at town meeting. I had no idea, however, of waiting for the town machinery to move. Mr. Cutter has already received instructions to furnish the whole company with such a uniform as you may decide upon; and if the town is not unanimous in a vote to pay the bill, I will cheerfully pay it myself."

The boys responded to this gratifying and wholly

unexpected announcement by giving three tremendous cheers for Squire Belmont. As the excitement somewhat subsided, it was observed that the squire frequently turned his eyes up the street, in the direction of his residence,˙ as if in expectation of some one from that quarter. Presently a smile of satisfaction came over his handsome face, and he turned to the captain of the Young Invincibles, and said,—

"To you, George, I wish to give some tangible proof of the˙ esteem in which I hold you for the faithful and judicious manner in which you have so long commanded your company, and more particularly for your prompt action last night, whereby a valuable ship has been saved to the government, and ten rascally pirates secured for the gallows — *I hope.*"

At this moment Squire Belmont's coachman rode up to the party on that gentleman's splendid young horse, " Speed." As the man dismounted, the squire took the horse by the bridle, patted him caressingly on his neck for a moment, and then led him along to George, saying, —

" Speed, I take much pleasure in introducing you to your new master, Captain George Herrick ; " and slipping the bridle over the youth's arm, the generous donor stepped back and rejoined Colonel White without another word.

For once, the lad appeared to be overcome by surprise. He stood for a few moments in silence, with his eyes fixed on the beautiful animal before him.

"George, hadn't you better thank the squire?" suggested Tom Sprightly. "Or shall *I* take the horse, and *do the thanks?*"

"I'm much obliged to you, Tom. You may *hold* the horse, but I think I'll try to thank our good friend myself;" and passing the bridle over to Tom, George approached the donor, and said, —

"Squire Belmont, this is a complete surprise to me; and I can only find words to say that I sincerely thank you for this most generous deed, and hope that I may in the future really *earn* a title to this magnificent present which you have prematurely bestowed upon me."

"I am perfectly willing to take your past conduct as a guarantee for the future," replied the squire, with a benevolent smile.

"Three more cheers for Squire Belmont!" cried Tom Sprightly, who was as much elated at his young friend's good fortune as he would have been to be the lucky recipient himself.

"As the sounds of the applause died away, the squire said, —

"Now, boys, three rousing cheers for your brave

young captain, whose first blow was for his *mother*, and his second for his *country!*"

The hearty response to this call was indisputable evidence of the high regard in which George Herrick was held, not merely by his immediate associates, but by the good people of the village at large — numbers of whom were assembled on the parade-ground as spectators to this pleasing little affair, and who most readily united their voices with those of the Invincibles in doing honor to the prompt, brave, and patriotic young commander.

Colonel White now stepped forward, and every sound was hushed in a moment.

"My esteemed young friends," began the old gentleman, "this is a happy occasion to us all. I congratulate you on your great advancement in military discipline, as well as for the favor and respect you have established for yourselves in the breasts of all good citizens by your orderly conduct and ready patriotism on all occasions. Contrast your present position with that of Jack Dunham! Had he taken an interest in his country's cause, as you have done, he might at the present time be happy and respected, instead of occupying a prison with rebel pirates! My boys, there is nothing like keeping a great and good object constantly in view.

"The munificence of our good friend here, the squire, has left nothing for me to offer but a few words of encouragement, which I have no doubt you will kindly receive from an old man who can now do little else than *talk*.

"I am happy to say that my expectations with regard to your military improvement have been more than realized. The interest and the spirit with which you entered into the movement, and which you have never allowed for a moment to flag, have resulted in honor to yourselves, and to the good old town of Harryseekit.

"You have set an example that is already being followed in other towns and states, and the subject of military instruction to boys has been broached, even, in some of the state legislatures. You have not only gained much useful military knowledge, but, by making *patriotism at home* your watchword, you have done much to strengthen love for the Union in older hearts — for men shame to falter when boys stand up in the front rank.

"My young friends, I come now to your crowning glory — the achievement of last night. It was a plan well conceived, and most admirably carried out. The result has stamped you as brave soldiers and true patriots, and brought you prominently to the notice of the government. I am satisfied that you are fully competent to act independently. Your present efficient officers need no further instruction from me. I am forced to admit, that, if I had been at home last evening, I should probably have advised a different course than the one pursued with regard to the defence of the General Grant. But no other course of action could have resulted any better; and the honor is all yours.

"My brave boys, I have only to add, Go on in your well doing. Be certain of the direction in which duty leads, and unhesitatingly follow it. You know •that my idea is, that no one under eighteen should enlist in the army. None of you have reached that age as yet; but I fear many of you will reach it before this terrible war is brought to a close. And there may possibly be a critical period in this great struggle when it will be necessary for government to throw overwhelming numbers suddenly into the field at some given point — in which case I might say 'Go' to some hardy youth who had not quite reached the standard age which I have set up.

"The hour has not *yet* come when the cause in the field really demands your assistance. In the mean time, continue your good efforts here. There is much more to be accomplished, both at home and in the

field, before peace will be restored. But wherever
duty points, there will be found, I feel well assured,
the Young Invincibles."

The perfect silence which had been maintained
during the feeling remarks of Colonel White continued for some moments after he ceased to speak. IIis
young friends' hearts were too full for cheers. Directly there was a simultaneous rush made by the
boys more closely around the kind old gentleman,
each one endeavoring to seize him by the hand or
arm, as if fearful lest their best friend and instructor
was about to withdraw his protecting shield from over
their heads. More than one eye gathered moisture
as the boys thus clung and hovered about him like
a swarm of bees.

Squire Belmont, thinking that this demonstration
of the boys might prove to be too much for his aged
friend, somewhat changed the scene by pointing towards the fence close by, which our old sailor friend
was just mounting, and suddenly calling out, —

" A speech from Uncle Bill ! "

The cry took with the crowd, and " A speech from
Uncle Bill ! " was so clamorously called for, that the
old seaman saw no way of escape, and, to use one
of his own favorite expressions, he decided to " heave
ahead."

"Boys," commenced Uncle Bill, taking off his hat and throwing it upon the ground, "if I was only on a ship's deck, and you were sailor lads, I should know just what to say; but, as it is, I s'pose I shall soon get out of my reck'ning.

"Well, my brave boys, as I sailed under your orders last night, I can testify that you run down upon the pirates handsomely on the windward tack, took the wind out of their sails, and cut them down to the water line when everything was shaking. The thing was done *shipshape*.

"Now, boys, *I'm* going to make a prophecy, — not a sixty days' one, — and that is, that the whole 'secesh' crew of the South will finally have to strike their colors to our forces, just as the pirates did to you last night; for, you see, they're in a condemned ship, they've thrown the safe old Union chart overboard, and they're sailing without a compass. So, you see, they'll just go round and round, land right where they started from, won't know their best friends, and — *will lose all their niggers !*"

Uncle Bill's speech "brought down the house," and lifted the oppression from the spirits of the boys.

Colonel White once more addressed the youthful throng, saying, —

"Do not for a moment think, my dear young

friends, that in taking leave of you as your instructor, I lose any of my interest in you individually or collectively. Far from it. So long as you continue true to our beneficent Father in heaven, to the Union, and to yourselves, you may count upon me as your stanch advocate and friend."

And here, kind reader, we must all, for the present, take our leave of the Young Invincibles and the other characters who have figured in the story. Perhaps strict justice to George Herrick's character demands of us at this time to say that there is no evidence to show that he has forgotten his silent, solemn pledge to Lizzie Swift beside the death-bed of her mother. Neither would we have the silence on the part of Lucy. White as regards her great indebtedness to Tom Sprightly interpreted to her disadvantage. So long as all these young persons themselves are true friends, less interested parties have no right to complain.

Should the indulgent reader feel sufficient interest in the "Young Invincibles" to follow their fortunes farther, it may result that "Patriotism at Home" was followed by Valor in the Field, thus showing The Success of True Merit.